The Broken Child

M.J.Wright

The Broken Child

Wright, M.J., author.

The broken child/M.J.Wright

ISBN: 9780994648105 Paperback

Notes: Includes index

Subjects: Future, The, in literature

 Romance fiction.

Book one of Elannas Children series.

Dewey Number: A823.4

Table of Contents

Acknowledgements:

Brooke, Catherine, Jaydhas and Marilee: Without your suggestions I would never have made it past the editing stages.

Rob: For the business advice.

My wonderful family,

For all the round robin amateur psychology hours. For the countless hours of listening to me talk characters, plot points and story arcs. Thank you for helping me weather the crazy days of writer's block. I love you both so very much.

To Mr Hoskings (*my eighth grade English teacher*),

You recognized talent in my writing and kept encouraging me for years after I stopped being your student. Without you this book would never have been started.

Thank you with all my heart.

M.

List of people and places.

Alek- a-lec-The name Mari gives Scott when they arrive back at the city meaning warrior of mankind.

Anna-The woman who successfully changed life for women for the better. Her rules and ideals keep most women safe from harm.

Anna's laws-The way a woman is raised and trained to treat men that they contract with.

Bordertown-The nearest town two days ride away from the energy harvesting farm the Jackson family live and work on.

Caged-Hidden away from the sight of all except for the one man a fifth is mated/contracted to.

Christiana a.k.a Tia-Liams mate. Mari attempts to save her life but she is too ill.

Contract-The legal paperwork that enables a man to have a monogamous relationship (de facto level) with a woman for a period of no less than five years. Male children stay with the father and female children are sent for training to the nearest city.

Eighter-A member of the territory of the way of the eight.

Elanna de Montmercy- E-lan-na-Mari's birthmother. Extremely manipulative.

Elder-A member of the public chosen to help govern the local populace and enforce Anna's rules.

Elder Bryce-A member of the high council who was Maris former tutor.

The Broken Child

Evan Hart-The current chief of the way of the eight. Liams father.

Fifth - A rare female who is born with all the innate traits that a woman should have and needs no training for the bedroom. Recognised by their purple hair. The lighter the colour the more precious the woman. These women are usually caged during their first contract. Valuable.

Half - A sole female in a contracted or mated relationship.

High council - The ruling council made up of elders from the elite families of the city.

Joanna Mercy - The foundling whom Mari took into Mercy House at the age of 12. Is Mari's personal assistant.

John Smythe - The contract Elanna forces Mari to finish on her behalf. He treated Mari as property and unsuccessfully tried to murder her. He successfully kills Elanna

Keilana - K-eye-lar-na - The little girl John uses to trick Mari with.

Kimana- k-eye-mar-na - The name Scott gives Mari when they arrive back to the city meaning beautiful butterfly.

Kimmi- Kim-mee - The diminutive of Kimana meaning my little butterfly.

Liam Hart - A former member and rightful chief of the way of the eight. Mari saves his life.

Marianna de Montmercy- M-ah-ri-ah-na - Mostly known as Mari. Contracts to the Jackson family. Also known as Lady Mercy and head of Mercy House.

Mate/mating - The ultimate commitment within a contract between a male and female that is a lifelong binding tie. Equal to marriage. All subsequent children are raised within this family unit. The female no longer has to cover her hair in deference to her mated status.

Mating marks - The tattoos a male and female receive at their commitment ceremony as an outward display of the binding promise between them. Each male designs the marks his female will wear for him alone. Mating marks are on display at all formal occasions.

Mercy House - Mari's home. Only rehabilitation centre in Spark City. It houses a hotel, ballet, fashion house, administration and office level, rehabilitation for battered women, orphanage and Mari's personal home in the penthouse.

Nicholas Jackson - Scott's father and mate to Susanna.

Oceania City - The dome city nearest the biggest known body of water. Susanna's daughter Liana lived there.

Owen Hart - Liams brother.

Quarter - A loose woman found in businesses set up to take care of male needs without contracts.

Rachael Saint - The woman Scott was courting seriously.

Rebekah Saint - An Elder of Bordertown. Scott was courting her daughter Rachael before she was murdered. Considers Scott her son.

Scott Jackson - Disillusioned son of Nick and Susanna. Lost the will to survive without Rachael when she died.

Spark City - The dome city Mari has resided in since birth. The dome closes out much of real nature.

Spirit woman/spirit fifth - A fifth so powerful in ley line energy that they manifest all the psychic abilities. Their hair turns blue

with violet strands through it during a huge expulsion of this
energy.

Susanna Jackson - Nick's mate and parent to Scott.

Third -A second female in a male/female relationship. Usually
requested by mated couples for the sole purpose of procreation
if the first female is unable to have children.

Prologue

The year is 2466. The earth has survived both social and environmental upheavals. In the year 2200 there were 500 males to every single female. Humanity was on the brink of disappearing altogether as major wars erupted. Females were treated no better than slaves to be bought and sold amongst the very rich.

The first high council had been created out of desperation. It had been led by a female named Anna and she demanded sweeping changes be made to society as a whole. Her laws became known as the laws of Anna.

The contract was brought into law as a way for a man to enter into a monogamous relationship with a single female for the sole purpose of procreation. Any daughters were sent to the city for education and any sons would be the sole property of their fathers. The minimum age for a contracted female was sixteen. All daughters would forever bear the name Anna somewhere in their names in tribute to the courageous woman who found a way to stop the killing.

Soon it became apparent that some couples wished to stay together past the initial five years of their contract. The mating ceremony was created soon after. It was a binding lifelong commitment symbolized with tattoos stretching around and up one arm of the body.

Most people now live within one of five dome cities. These are linked together by two trains. Nature has taken over the unclaimed areas. All traces of the past have disappeared and the land has returned to being as wild as it was before mankind tamed it. These large areas are known as the territories.

Those living in the territories still follow the old ways. All those who are found guilty of crimes against humanity are turned loose within the territories. If they can survive for the span of a contract their crimes are forgiven but they are never forgotten.

There is also still a rogue element who see females as nothing more than possessions. Those who are careful to hide their personal views survive on the outer edges of society usually running their businesses in the slum areas of the cities on the outer rim known as the rim tenements.

Chapter One - Marianna de Montmercy

'Do you think that makes any difference?' she asked her reflection gesturing to the walking stick leaning up against the wall beside her. Marianna had asked herself the same question every day for the last eight years. Her answer had never differed. The stick hadnt changed her perception of herself. The reason behind her needing one had all but made her an invisible.

At thirty years old she was easily still one of the most exquisite females to grace Spark City. Her silver eyes regarded her appearance thoughtfully. She was dressed to blend into the background so that she would not be noticed. All except for her lavender hair with white streaks interspersed throughout the strands. Her hair and the luminosity of her eye colour attracted unwanted attention.

Her official classification was a fifth. Her unofficial classification was the highest number in society. She was regarded as being amongst the rarest of females and had been provided with more security than she was comfortable with by the high council. It was rumoured that Mari had more security attached to her than even Anna herself.

She hated the term invisible with every fibre of her being. Mari could not change the circumstances behind her injuries. She had taken to heart the life lessons she had learnt during her healing process to change the lives of many others like her from the city and surrounding rim tenements. She closed her eyes for a few moments and concentrated solely on her breathing. When she opened her eyes she reached out for the book on the coffee table in front of her.

Contained inside was the account of the darkest moments of her life. Each year on the 5th of May, as day turned to night and the stars began to appear over the dome Marianna re-membered. She remembered the letter she received from her mother urging her to visit her so that they could meet. She remembered the cold calculating looks that she received when-ever Elanna had thought she wasn t paying attention. Mari remembered with cold clarity meeting John Smythe and the way he had made her feel as he kissed the back of her hand with his dry lips.

Next came shock when Elanna informed her that she would be completing the contract with John on her mother s behalf. Dis-belief as she realised she had been drugged to be compliant by something in her food. Elanna herself had guided her hand as she had made her sign the substitution clause.

Some of her most agonizing memories were gone from her mind and the healers had explained that when it was needed the relevant information would be there. Only when she was truly ready to deal with what had happened to her. Until then she would be forever slightly broken.

The next few months after she had been manipulated into sign-ing the agreement were a fleeting montage of pain and over-whelming emotions as she struggled in an unfamiliar environ-ment dealing with a male who had no inclination to do anything but issue orders at her. Mari picked up the glass of whiskey that had sat untouched beside the book. She took a mouthful and savoured the taste before she swallowed it down.

She flipped the pages with one hand as she came to the sketches that depicted her eighteenth season. The year she knew she would have etched indelibly in her memory for the rest of her life.

She had been with child for the very first time when John had sent her flying over a third floor balcony using the momentum from a well-placed kick to her chest. She had died and lost her child during her fight for life in the tense hours soon after. Mari could remember a visit from the leader of the high council only known to one and all as Madame Speaker. The female had seemed genuinely distressed for her beneath her heavy veils of navy blue.

She had shared the silence with Mari allowing her to grieve in peace. Mari took another mouthful of whiskey as she held up her glass to the picture of the woman who had forsaken her duties to run the nation in order to hold her hand. At least before her red entourage had arrived to callously inform Mari that her mother had been found murdered by Johns hands.

Justice had been swift and she had not seen John again. He had been shipped to the territories in the clothes he had been wearing and not much by the way of supplies. It had been assumed by society at large that he had not survived as he had not returned at the end of five years to resume his life. Marianna had not been as easily convinced.

She had just finished her last round of operations, healing sessions and intense physical therapy on the leg that had shattered at an odd angle in an effort to save her unborn child. Mari put down her empty glass with the silent hope that her child was happy wherever she was in the cycle of life. She closed the book and blew a birthday kiss into the cosmos.

Mari moved slowly to the picture window overlooking the city. The high council building was lit up artistically as usual and her silver eyes darkened to a stormy grey. The high council had thrown her to the society sharks after she was mostly healed.

Where she had once been treated with respect, men attempted to take liberties with her without contracting with her for her time. Mari had appealed to the high council for their protection.

It had come at a heavy cost. She had effectively gone from being one man's captive to being at the mercy of the high council. In order for their protection, she had to pay a large percentage of any profits from any business venture for the rest of her life. She had reluctantly agreed to any and all terms.

In secret she had begun weapons training. She had known then and still believed quite heavily that the only reason the high council had treated her so favourably was because Madame Speaker had taken a liking to her. The Elders saw Mari as a threat of some sort. She had worked hard learning how to best support her body and move with grace while wielding a knife. She was deadly accurate with her stick and completely lethal with throwing knives.

Mari had kept more than a close eye on the movements at Smythe Towers where she had been held captive for all those years. She had a gut feeling that John was still alive somewhere in the territories. The man was black to his very soul. She knew he would not rest once he found out that Mari had survived her fall.

As she was walking past an alley one morning she came across a child who had been beaten within an inch of death simply because she had been late home from training. Mari had taken her home on the spot and arranged to have her medical bills sent to her. That one child had been the catalyst to her seeing the others that blended into the hidden places in misplaced shame.

Mari returned to the high council with a proposal. At first she thought that she would be laughed out of the audience room by the Elder who had stared incredulously at her. Surprisingly she had ushered her through to the inner chambers to be heard by Madame Speaker herself.

Her proposal had been quite simple. If she found a female who had been abandoned, hurt or needed help she would offer them sanctuary within her home. The children would be raised with the correct training afforded all the females under Anna's laws and at in their sixteenth season they would be able to choose whether they wished to contract or not.

If they did and Mari was approached about one of them she would act in the best interest of the female. She would have the potential choosing fully investigated so that she could guarantee her charges ongoing safety. For those who did not wish to contract Mari would train to be useful in the running of the building. Any adult females that she found broken would be offered medical and emotional assistance as well as a home for as long as they needed one.

She wished to turn her home de Montmercy House into a refuge. She had left the high council feeling at peace with herself for the first time in a very long time. Mercy House as her home was now known currently housed over thirty children, twenty females who lived in the rehabilitation centre and her home on the top floor.

Mari leaned up against the glass. She had slowly lost herself in the day to day intricacies of helping those who needed her. Spark City had forgotten Marianna de Montmercy existed and to the world at large she was now simply known as Lady Mercy. She had all but disappeared and it was only once a year on this day that she allowed herself the opportunity to remember and heal a little more.

The sharp tone of her com pierced through the silence. She wished that she could ignore it. She knew that she could not. The message was from her personal assistant Joanna.

'All quiet downstairs. I m turning in for the night. Need anything?'

Mari replied quickly with a short

'No thanks. See you in the morning.'

She had found Joanna out in the Rim, dragging her small frame along the street with blood dripping steadily from a series of puncture wounds around her back kidney area. She had been determined to make it to the only healing centre in the area without help from any one. The street had all but been deserted when Mari had caught her as she had fallen. She had arranged to have her transferred to Mercy House after they had patched her together and the child had needed somewhere safe to go.

Jo had been insistent about her freedom from the minute she had awoken in strange surroundings. Mari had assured her that no one would ever take that away from her. In Mercy House every one was afforded their freedom-everyone except Mari herself who could not shake the eyes of the high council. One morning she had been waiting for Mari in her office and had told her she had needed her help. Jo had started speaking and made so much sense that she had ended up staying on as her personal assistant. That had been over four seasons ago.

She had turned into the beauty who had refused to be tamed completely. Jo had retained the wildness of a street child underneath the guise of a well-trained female. Once in a while she would slip up and mention her family of brothers who had kept her safe. Mari knew Jo still visited them whenever time allowed.

Mari moved away from the window as the glass had grown cool along with the evening air. The rage she usually kept contained behind a cool icy exterior bubbled up from deep within. Mari gasped and clutched her stomach. The white hot pain clutched her insides with sharp hooks. Something wet slipped over her cheek. Reaching up with her fingers she realised with a start she was crying.

Bubbles of insane laughter rose from the uncomfortable feeling from deep within. She clutched her mouth frantically trying to push herself back from teetering on the edge of the insanity that was her life.

Chapter Two - Nick and Susanna

They had come to the city with one purpose in mind and that was to find their son a chosen. The life they led out in the territories would ask much of a city female. They had to be sure whomever they approached would be able to survive the isolation amongst other things.   Numbness had set in not long after the despondency.

The heaviness of his arm across her shoulders had kept her firmly entrenched in the present. A grey fog clouded her thought pattern. It was if they sat on a hard bench surrounded by a mini dome. Trapped. Strangers. Unable to communicate their true needs to the females walking past. The different colours whirled in front of her eyeballs at night. Lost. She felt lost in a sea of strangers. Despite the beauty that surrounded them no one stopped to take a breath.

Susanna had not been trained in Spark City. She had completed her training in Oceania. The atmosphere had been more relaxed and all females could be easily identified by the colour of their wrist bands. She inhaled a deep breath and as she silently released the air she released a small prayer of hope along with it.

She turned to the man seated beside her. It had been quite

some time since their choosing and she wanted reassurance from him that they were making the right decision. Her mate's face broke into the easy grin he reserved just for her. 'He cannot live in the past for all of time. Its time to bring him to life.' His words were for her ears alone as he continued to scan their surroundings for threats.

It was in that moment that they both looked up to witness Mari slowly limp across the grass in her bare feet. She stood still leaning heavily on her stick as she gazed aimlessly across the lake. Susanna hid a small smile as she observed Mari wriggling her toes in obvious delight at her small rebellion. Her joy was evident in her face for all to see and it was then that Susanna knew she was the one. 'I want to speak with her.' She was already rising to make the introduction. 'Not here.' Her mate reminded her, 'Too public.' He watched them collide and heard Susanna apologise for her clumsiness. The same clumsiness that had allowed her to place a tracker in the female's bag.

A few nights later Mari felt a tap against her walking stick as a male voice asked her the question she asked herself daily, 'Do you think that makes any difference?' She raised her eyes from the dancers gathering on the stage below her private box. Her expression was one of interest as she recognised the couple who had been in the park watching her take time to breathe in her busy schedule. They had positioned themselves to her right which made her more than a little uncomfortable.

Mari half wondered if they were waiting for her to scream. No one had ever invaded her personal space in the concert hall before. She was intrigued by the bold move and as she moved to the chair in the corner so she could observe them she wondered if the collision had been nothing more than a set up. Mari continued to politely wait for their next words. Her brow wrinkled fleetingly as she tried to remember if she had read a report lately of one of the girls intending to contract. She was used to being approached on their behalf but this time she had had no prior warning.

The couple sitting silently in front of her were not from the cities. He had been too forward in his approach not using any of the polite speech she was used to and his hands were work roughened. She took note of the way he moved as if he was used to dealing with wide open spaces more than the close quarters of a city building. Mari turned her gaze to the female seated beside him. She was dressed in an outfit of Oceania City origin that looked to be more than a year old. No city female dared keep their clothing past six months.

She was fairly sure they had come from the territories in search of a chosen. It looked as if the lucky female would be kept in comfort. Mari had glimpsed mating marks peeking out of their vintage leather jackets. Only the wealthy could afford to keep leather jackets as family heirlooms. Rumor had it that once diamonds were once as valuable. But after the collapse food was valuable, good warm clothing was valuable and to have or be a female was wealth beyond measure.

She looked at the female's tattoo again noticing how it encircled her heart finger then wrapped itself around her hand and arm as if it were caressing her. The marks the man sported were tribal in nature and if her memory served her correctly male mating marks were dual purpose if you knew what you were looking for. It was rumoured that the males outside cities marked their lineage on their bodies so they would never forget where they had come from.

As the silence lengthened she waited patiently. 'I could have a weapon!' The male's statement unnerved her but with all the safety measures she had in place she found it highly unlikely. Chances were they would have had to check all weapons at the first cloak room. She knew that weapons were easily concealed. 'Do you?' Mari could be just as direct considering no security measures were completely fail safe. The female exhaled softly sounding annoyed. They had invaded her private space. Her security team would need to be briefed as soon as she had finished with the couple. She raised her eyes to their faces and asked again for emphasis, Do you?' She searched their faces for the answer when they did not answer verbally.

Mari watched the couple exchange a long look and concluded that the threat of weapons had been intended to throw her off balance. 'This is no place to discuss contracts. If you would like to follow me.' She rose to her feet steadily. She took them to the private reception room just off the front desk. Jo appeared at her elbow and quietly cleared her throat. 'I have some business to attend to. Could you please have tea served?' showing her guests a serene look on her face she turned back to the girl beside her, 'Then privacy for the rest of the evening I think. If any urgent reports come in have Lilli place them on my desk in my personal office upstairs.'

She followed the couple into the room waited until the female was seated and then sat once again with her back to the wall. 'Welcome to Mercy House. Who is it that you were hoping to contract with?' Mari spoke in a gentle tone. She clasped her hands together in her lap and as she waited for the couple to answer her Jo appeared with the tea service used for contract discussions. As she served the tea she shot Mari a sympathetic look. Using their private security gestures Mari indicated that she would talk to her before the end of the night. Jo bowed her head slightly to their guests then quietly shut the door behind her with a click.

She wished she could make them feel more at ease with her. 'We have not spoken the formal words of the contract ritual yet.' She began softly, 'I know that this is breaking etiquette but I wish to put you at your ease. My name is Marianna de Montmercy.' She poured the tea and placed the cups in front of the strangers on the round table between them. As she finished serving herself the female spoke, 'I am Susanna Jackson and this is my mate Nicholas. As you can tell this is not easy for us. The female we wished to approach is you.'

Mari remained quiet allowing her to continue as she watched Nicholas's face. She had already been contracted once and they were mated. She had a feeling that there was something larger motivating the couple than their own pleasure or wish for children.

The idea of the contract had become slightly outdated over the last two centuries. Once it had been the only legal way for a male to spend quality time with a female. That aspect of it hadn't changed. What had changed was the fact that one contract was no longer limited to couples. Triads were forming and in some circles males were abusing the legal system in order to keep harems.

'How long have you been watching me?' behind Mari's calm exterior she was suspicious. Loss of control at this point would not help matters. No one offered for her. The stick was enough to scare everyone away. People had stopped seeing her unless they wanted something from her. From Mercy House. Her eyes widened slightly. White noise filled her ears as she dealt with her confusion. Her thoughts were swirling. Susanna's voice cut through the emotional fallout, 'Long enough. Will you at least hear us?' Mari bowed her head as if in thought as she regained her calm.

'You are an uncontracted female of eligible age. Your manners are lovely however your sense of self-preservation is sorely undeveloped.' Nicholas spoke as if he had had her followed. Mari knew that it was extremely difficult to do since she was guarded both day and night. The legal words had been spoken and she had no other option left to her other than to hear them out. 'Before we begin is there not another who we should approach about this?' Susanna's quiet demeanour and thoughtfulness showed an understanding of both the contract and the ritual surrounding it.

The ritual surrounding the contract was as important if not more important than the legal document they would sign if they were all happy with the terms they had agreed upon. The unsaid words could sometimes be heard as clearly as the spoken ones. The tea ritual was a time where they could speak the truth without fear of recrimination. Hearing the truth of someone was something no one took for granted anymore. The world had become one giant struggle for power and fortune.

Mari chose her words carefully, 'You know that I am more than of age. You will know that there is no one else. I will hear you but no promises are binding until I am satisfied.' Definitely no backing out now. She knew she would have to wait for explanations on why they had chosen to approach her specifically. Susanna dipped her head in acknowledgement of her assessment of the situation.

'We would like you to be our contracted third or our son Scotts contracted half.' Susanna spoke again. Every female was presented with a choice between family members. The contract had been designed to help females feel as if they had some choice in a very untenable position. A third was the third person in a triad usually because a mated couple were incapable of having children. A true third was hard to keep and even harder to entice. Mari had heard of triad matings but they were incredibly rare and still considered on the outer fringes of acceptance in society.

Mari wondered if they were willing to overlook her specific needs in order to lure her out from under the dome. It was the way of the world that the elders in the family houses played chess with the lives of their children in order to gain position, power and more money. She had just never heard of any one approaching an invisible before to offer them the same concessions as a normal female.

She took another sip of tea and waited with that blank serene look all women were taught especially for the negotiations surrounding something as important as a contract. 'I'm sure you have many questions for me.' she spoke into the silence that had stretched on for far too long. She looked at her hands the skin almost translucent in the light and realised that they would need to see more of her to get a true idea of what she really looked like. Only mated females were permitted to have their hair uncovered both in public and at home.   Mari unpinned her head wrap but left it draped over her hair. She still had very fuzzy images of how this next bit had gone in her last pre contract negotiations. Her body tensed at the bad memory. 'Please feel free to veto what you are not comfortable with answering.' Susanna looked at Nick in confusion. He raised a questioning brow but indicated that they should continue. It would depend on the questions asked of her Mari thought. She could not by law just volunteer information at this point. She had to wait for the questions. This put her slightly on edge because she had no wish to delve into the memories that were best left forgotten.

'You have been contracted before?' Most females her age had been contracted three or four times by the age of thirty. Mari knew the implications behind the question was more did she know what would be expected of her. 'Yes.' Her voice was soft but steady so Susanna continued, 'What is your designated level?'

There were five levels in the laws of Anna that all females were categorised into. Females in levels one and two were expected to train for work other than contracting. Levels three and four had a high chance of multiple contracts that might lead to a mating. Any females categorised a level five had been born into their label. These females had purple hair and usually displayed some kind of uncanny skills. The phrase used to describe them was a chance to touch heaven here on earth. Fifths were usually mated during their first contract and then caged immediately.

'I am a fifth.' Mari took a sip of tea. She was one of the most precious females in the world. She knew that this was one of the major reasons the High Council had assigned her a security detail at all times. She herself had had the cameras installed throughout her building. She allowed them time to absorb the shock of her answer before adding, 'Please continue.' She tried to sound encouraging. 'Your contract?' Nick leaned forward in his seat. Mari heard his unasked questions of *What happened and why were you let go?*

'It was completed with no renewal on my part. He…' Mari's voice stumbled and her eyes filled with unshed tears, 'he was not kind.' She had been manipulated, used, brutalised and then left for dead. She looked down at her now empty cup and used the time to recompose herself. She raised her eyes to see how Nick and Susanna had received her comment. Nick had an extremely black look on his face and his fingers were slightly curled on the table top as if he was in the process of making a fist. Susanna had frozen in her spot.

Mari rose from her seat and left her stick in the corner. She limped over to the stack of wraps she kept in a cane basket on top of an antique wooden filing cabinet. Susanna was showing the markers of a female who had been through an ordeal of her own. Mari lifted the top wrap off the pile and gently draped one over Susanna's upper body for extra warmth. Unobtrusively she gave a nod to the camera indicating she may need help soon. She knew that they wouldn t rush the room unless she was physically being threatened. Nothing could be accomplished until Susanna became responsive and Nick calmed himself.

She could understand Nick's anger but as much as she appreciated his outrage on her behalf her past had already happened. Their society was mostly a peaceful one. Crimes against humanity were dealt with swiftly. Mari had been told that John Smythe had so greatly angered Madame Speaker that she had had him killed.

Mari poured them all a fresh cup of tea. She wrapped Susanna's hands around her cup and urged softly, 'Drink.' She placed Nick's in front of him carefully. His anger was like a palpable entity in the room and if she left him in it much longer she feared that it would grow out of proportion.

She took a sip of her tea contemplating her words before she finally spoke to him. ' Your anger cannot change my past.' Her words seemed to have the intended affect. Susanna took a sip of her tea then put down the cup. Nick's hands flattened on the table before he looked at his mate. He cleared his throat before speaking, 'It will not happen again. My son and I, we do not hurt females. You will be safe with us.' His dark eyes held the truth of his promise.

Mari nodded again to the camera indicating that the security team should stand down. 'Susanna and I had a clause built into our contract that if broken renders the whole contract void. We can promise you the same concession. If a hand is lifted against you in anger you will be free to leave and we will present ourselves to the High Council for justice.' Nick looked at Susanna, 'It helped us to build trust when there was no reason for any to be had.'

A safety clause. Trust. She could only nod wordlessly in agreement. Anger. His anger had been in her defense. Her brow wrinkled. No one had ever been angry on her behalf before. Nick's words had touched her. Mari truly felt at a loss on how to respond. 'Your comfort is a priority for us.' Susanna sounded reassuring as she added, 'The extra warmth was most thoughtful. Its a beautiful wrap. Can you tell me where I can buy one?' Mari could feel a smile creep across her face in response to Susanna's statement. 'If you like it-then it is yours.' She replied. The wrap was one of her own designs that had been made up in the fashion rooms as a training exercise.

Mari removed her head wrap to real her lavender hair with white streaks through it. She folded it neatly beside her allowing the-couple to confirm that she had indeed been born a fifth of the highest level. Stunned Susanna asked softly, 'Is that?' 'Natural,' Mari confirmed already used to the question having heard it from other females. She added 'However if colour is an issue...'

'You need not change it.' Nick stopped her, 'Unless we are at home it will stay covered.'

Mari waited until Susanna explained, 'This contract should you agree will take you outside the dome city into the territories. Your hair is a unique color and will not blend into nature well. Our enemies would see you coming before you would see them.' Mari could see that she was curious when she asked, 'How long is it?'

'My braid reaches below my knees. Unbound it is much longer.' Mari started to remove the pins from her elaborate hairstyle. She glanced over at Nick through her lashes and he nodded for her to continue. She unwound her hair until it was a simple plait that swung free. Her fingers grazed the binding at the bottom as she pulled it forward over her shoulder. She took another sip of tea and waited for their next question

Chapter Three - Deep within the ritual

'Forgive us for asking but do you have daughters to care for?'
Mari knew that this was way outside the realms of standard
questioning when it came to the contract. She could appreciate the thought that had gone into such a sensitive question.
Not many people would consider the offspring of a female they
wished to contract with. 'My children are the children of Mercy
House.' Mari kept her answer short and then asked, 'Will that
be a requirement of this contract?' With her heartbeat thrumming in her ears she waited to hear their answer. Mari wasnt
sure why they had asked the question but she hoped her shock
had not transmitted to her face for them to read.

'You have never given birth?' Susanna's voice held a note of
concern. Mari lowered her gaze to her hands on the table
clasped together so hard that her knuckles were turning white.
She took a deep breath before replying, 'I was in a horrendous
accident. The child I was carrying at the time was lost and the
healers could not give me any assurances that I would be able
to in the future.' Mari was not ashamed of her bodys inadequa-
cies.

'Could you elaborate on the circumstances surrounding the
accident? We can decide the relevancy of children to this con-

tract from there.' Susanna shot a warning glance at Nick. Mari caught it and wondered if his anger was volatile enough that it would scare her into signaling for security again. She felt as if she was slowly curling inside herself to dig deep for the memories that were best buried forever.

Mari observed Nick flicking his eyes from Susanna to the door. Susanna nodded once in response. As they both gave Mari their full attention she realized that Nick would remove himself from the room if his anger threatened to spill over into words. Mari knew she was broken but she was not beyond repair. They would have to give her time to deal with whatever situation they were attempting to bring her into. Mari took herself back to the season of her sixteenth summer. She had spent the last few seasons learning how to be pleasing in every single way. Then that note arrived with summons from her mother. 'I was contracted at sixteen as is usual.' Mari rose stiffly and circled the table.

She watched as Nick tracked her movements with his eyes and Susanna sipped her tea giving her the time she needed to find the words. The horror of her past hit her anew as she remembered how she had been given five minutes with her mother after she had signed the contract. The females who had led her from the room had stripped her of her clothing, dressed her in a silk shift and led her to the room that would be her cage. 'I was caged. For three years my whole world was narrowed down to one room and an ensuite.' Her eyes said more than her words, 'In the fourth year I was to give birth.'

Mari could remember it as clearly as if it had been yesterday. She had been so excited and had spent hours singing to her belly when there was no summons on her body. She closed her eyes. A tear tracked its way down her face. 'If this is too difficult... ' Susanna began half rising to soothe her. Mari watched as Nick shook his head at her. Mari squared her shoulders as she felt the onslaught of her worst memories slightly overwhelming her. Susanna poured herself more tea and waited patiently.

'I'm sorry. I just needed a moment. The words don t always come easily.' Mari took the cup that Nick offered her. She took a deep gulp of the liquid as she semi composed herself. She continued in a halting voice, 'I was pushed face first from a third floor balcony. I barely survived the impact of the fall. I lost my child because of it. I spent the next two years in and out of healing centers. My healing consisted of multiple operations and intense therapy sessions. After completing the scheduled therapy the healers still could not give me any future guarantees that I would be able to carry another child.'

Mari mentally shook off the fog of her past memories and opened her eyes. It still felt like it had been just yesterday and she remembered why she chose to only spend one day a year in remembrance of her daughter. A quick movement in front of her helped her to focus on the present as she heard the door click. Nick had left the room.

She took another deep cleansing breath. Mari felt tired, wrung out and a little out of sorts. She hoped she would not have to repeat her whole story to Nick and Susanna's son if she chose to take the contract. She made her way back to her seat then poured herself another cup of tea. 'How did you survive?' Susanna's whispered question indicated that the night's business had concluded. Mari regarded her thoughtfully, 'I was not given any other option.' She had had no choice really. The healers had dragged her kicking and screaming back into her body.

She began to coil her braid up and repin her hair into the elaborate style she had started the evening out with. There was one thing preying on her mind. One question that had yet to be answered. 'Will you require the full preview tomorrow night?' she asked before raising her head wrap.

Mari hoped not. This was something she highly discouraged whenever she was advocating on behalf of one of the Mercy House girls. She had found the experience to be highly humiliating as if she was a high bred mare who had been thoroughly inspected. 'If I said yes?' Nick leaned against the door jamb with an eyebrow raised startling her out of her thoughts. She thought he seemed calm enough but she kept her distance just to be on the safe side.

Mari watched as Nick shut the door gently and then heard the click as he locked it. He came no closer as she processed the slight alarm that rang through her body. She was thankful for his consideration but knew he was testing her. This was the usual pre contract game of chicken.

'Then I would have to comply as you well know.' Mari slowly removed her head wrap and dropped it on the floor. Her hair pins soon followed it-their tinkling sounds the only noise in the room. Mari swiftly uncoiled and unbraided her hair. She peeked up through her lashes at Nick. Raw hunger was etched on his face. If he wanted to play a game of chicken she would oblige him.

Mari stood and used the back of a chair for balance. Her long fall of hair rippled down her back as smooth as silk. 'No one will disturb us for the rest of the night.' She spoke in a calm voice. Mari kept her eyes trained on Nicks face and her discomfort in the idea of being naked in front of strangers buried deep.

In the old days the preview was one of the deeper parts of the ritual. It signified a female's willingness to please her contract. It showed the female the true motives behind a male's approach for her. If he was serious about not mistreating her he wouldnt handle her roughly. If not Mari had heard the horror stories whispered down through the ages of females who had suffered everything short of the actual joining between a male and female.

She felt Susanna's fingers in her hair fingering the strands of hair gently. As she cupped the back of her head Mari could feel her mouth close to her ear. 'You have given much of yourself already tonight.' Susanna's voice had turned sultry as her hand ran lightly over her arm. Mari could feel the warmth of Susanna's mouth move away from her ear. Her fingers gently disengaged themselves from Mari's hair and Mari heard her take soft steps backward.

She saw the moment Nick decided to approach her. He moved fluidly like one of the big cats she had read about. Mari squared her shoulders determined not to let him intimidate her in any way. This was her house. She had not been this close to a male since the night on the balcony. She shivered involuntarily and watched as he stopped less than a pace away from her. She felt him tip her face up gently so he could read the emotions behind her eyes. She hoped she had buried everything she was feeling deep behind a wall of courage thicker than steel.   Mari felt him circle around behind her before he moved back into her view. She felt him run a finger down her face following the track of an involuntary tear.

'No. We will not require preview.' His voice was extraordinarily gentle as he continued speaking, 'This is not a standard con- tract. Your willing demonstration was more than enough. We are from the territories and do not believe that our females should be put through such a barbaric practice. As enticing as you are you may keep your dignity siren.'

Siren. No one had called her that in a very long time. A siren was irresistible to all who heard her voice and saw her. She low- ered her gaze as she spoke softly, 'Until tomorrow night then.' Mari kept her gaze firmly focused on the floor until she heard the door shut. She focused on her breathing until her heart was beating normally again. Her fingers worked quickly to tame her mass of hair back into a single braid. When she raised her eyes to sweep the room she noticed a single card on the table with the words, *Same place tomorrow* in masculine scrawl.

Mari felt unsettled as once again the memory of the night be- fore rose like a specter to haunt her thought process. She had felt the lure of desire rising between them. Susanna"s tender touch on her skin had made her feel beautiful-wanted. Nick's hot gaze had swept her from head to toe. Emotions she had no labels for swirled through her body and she shook her head in frustration.

The prospect of a contract with this family both disturbed and-intrigued her at the same time. The Jacksons had been so mys terious with their approach she wondered if they were running-from something themselves. Nick had anger issues and Susan-na had been hurt very badly. Mari knew she had to think logi-cally about the situation before she listened to her gut feelings.

This contract would have to be more than about the monetary compensation if she was to leave Mercy House for the territories for the next five years. She rubbed her temple with her fingers.

A light headache was settling in as she felt swamped by all the details she would have to have organized before meeting with them again that evening. Mari stood up and stretched out the stiffness in her leg and back. She had the wellbeing of every-one under her roof to consider. How could she be selfish with the future of the females she had made promises to?

'You want to know what I think?' Jo was framed in her doorway her arms full of the files Mari had asked her to retrieve from the filing room. 'Of course.' Mari took her seat again waving Jo into one across the desk from her. When they were both com-fortable Jo spoke again, 'I think you need to make a change. You haven t been living for yourself since the accident and circumstances have trapped you into being tied to Mercy House without reprieve.' 'I'm scared.' Mari admitted. Silver eyes met electric blue as Jo spoke gently, 'Life is scary boss. Time to join the adventure again. What do you need from me so that you can do this?'

'I need you to do my job.' Mari spoke as she thought through everything that would be needed keep Mercy House running. She watched as her friend nodded, 'The real question you need to ask yourself is not whether or not I can do your job but do you trust me enough to let go?' All vestiges of Jo s previous life on the streets seemingly melted away. Mari felt as if she had changed from the adorable stubborn street urchin into a capable female in that instant.

'I trust you to take care of them. Anything you cant handle or needs my signature will have to be sent to me until we can sort out something more permanent.' Mari did not hesitate with her answer. The only problems she could foresee would be with the heads of the departments who were all used to dealing with her alone. 'I'll organize a full meeting for all the heads in an hour.' Jo anticipated her next request easily and gave her a reassuring smile.

'Just let them know that they dont have a vote on my final decision about this contract.' Mari piled the stack of folders in front of her. She watched Jo softly closing her door. With her friend in charge she knew that the girls would be looked after with the same level of care and training while she was away. Mari headed up to the penthouse at the end of the meeting feeling tired. Her leg was in excruciating agony. She watched the long afternoon shadows creep across the square in front of Mercy House as she rested in preparation for the evening to come.

Resting a notebook on her lap she began to write the questions she would be asking the couple. When she was finished Mari watched the light fade as she rose to change her outfit. The second half of the ritual was more formal than the first. Finally ready she slipped her second earring in her ears and then settled her head wrap over her hair. It was time and she could no longer hold off making a decision.

Chapter Four - Final Negotiations

After waiting for confirmation from security that her private box in the concert hall was empty Mari sat down with her back to the wall in preparation for her guests. She had not liked the fact that she had left herself open to sneak attacks the previous night. 'You need anything before I turn in for the night?' Jo asked as she poked her head around the curtain. Mari shook her head, 'The meeting room is set up. I dont anticipate being here for too long.' Jo reached out and took her hand. She squeezed it lightly before leaving Mari to her thoughts.

Mari hid a small smile as she listened to the children fidgeting as usual before the performance. Swan Lake was full of technical footwork but with society structured in such a way. Everyone older who was capable to dance in it was either in a contract or surviving the best way they knew how. She focused on the children, again taking note of those who had tuned everything out but the part they were about to dance.   Mari missed the way her body had moved before her ordeal. She had been a dancer with incredible flexibility.

She closed her eyes and focused on the whispered conversations floating up from the seats on the floor level. Speculation was alive about who the mysterious Lady Mercy could be. As with other nights she had to suppress the urge to have a good belly laugh more than a number of times. She had heard the words saint so many times coupled with the word spirit that she was of the opinion that it was the ghost of Anna herself walking the streets again.

She wore the grey hooded cloaks every time she left the building so that no one would remember the female who had rescued a child's life. Over the years the mythology behind Lady Mercy had grown to astonishing heights. Mari had even been chased by those who had wished to find out her identity.

'Will you hear us?' she heard Nick ask in a low voice. Mari's gaze swung around to the couple who seemed to appear and disappear like shades themselves. She could see that they had dressed formally with their mating marks on full display. Susanna had her chestnut braid intricately coiled and Nick was clean shaven. His shaggy blond hair was groomed neatly while her nails had been manicured and were the colour she imagined the ocean to be. Mari had also dressed formally in a choosing dress of mid blue with a matching head wrap. 'Will you hear me? she countered softly.

The tiny dancers were all business now as the night's performance was beginning. Mari gracefully led the way to a meeting room on the business level. This room was more comfortable than the one they had used the night before to start the negotiations. Inside it contained three wing backed chairs, side tables, a low table between them all and a footrest. The sideboard held a range of finger foods and the requisite tea. 'This is most thoughtful.' Mari watched as Susanna sat first. She seemed to be charmed by the seating arrangement. 'I wished for you to be comfortable. We may be here for quite some time tonight.' Mari said as she removed her head wrap and draped it over the chair with the footrest.

She poured the tea for her guests before seating herself. She made sure everything they needed for the duration of the negotiations was already in the room before she spoke the ritual words, 'Please begin I am ready to hear you.' She waited patiently as Susanna and Nick exchanged looks. She watched Nick lean forward to rest his elbows on his knees before he asked her the same question he led with the night before, 'Do you think that makes any difference to how you are treated in life?'

Mari wondered at the significance of the question and what piece of information they were hoping to gain about her by reiterating it again. She knew that it was easy to hide behind needing help instead of living her life for herself. Mari raised her eyebrow at him. They were trying to see inside her head as well as hear the truth of her. Maybe the information they sought was important for the environment they lived in. Or maybe they were still trying to work out how damaged she was and whether she was worth the risk of contracting with.

'May I clarify the question? Are you asking if people treat me differently? Or if I let it affect me to the point of hiding from life?' She chose to answer the heart of his question rather than give something that wasn t needed. Nick replied, 'Do people treat you differently?' He took a piece of fruit off the plate in front of him and bit into it while waiting for her to answer.

'People in the city do not know how to handle an imperfection in a female. I do not know how it is outside but here I became invisible to them a long time ago.' Mari wished she could convey the frustrations she felt on the subject to them more honestly but this was not the time or place. Susanna changed the subject, 'You have only been contracted just the once then?' Mari smiled a wry smile, They do not see me to even think of offering for me anymore.' There was no bitterness in her voice only acceptance.

'Their loss may be our gain.' Nick spoke again. Mari heard the tone in his voice reminding her that they saw her as more than just her walking stick. Susanna phrased her next question very carefully, 'How did Mercy House as you call it come into being?' Mari guessed that like most travellers through Spark City

all they had heard about her home was the surface rumours.
There were three of these. She had started them herself in a
citywide game of chinese whispers in an effort for those who
needed help to come find her themselves.

'Mercy House welcomes people from all walks of life. We have
no class designations here. Both genders are welcome on the
first four floors but to guarantee peace of mind for those in
my care only females and my personal guests may access the
upper levels. On these are the rehab and healing centre, the
children s quarters and classrooms then on the top floor is my
personal quarters. ' Mari had guided them out of the concert
hall modelled on the concert halls of their ancient past. She
had been with them when they had ridden in the glass elevator
for the first time. From inside it she had watched Susanna cran-
ing her neck as she had caught glimpses of the fashion rooms
and the hotel.

Mari raised her eyes and looked them full in the face, 'I told you
last night that when I was tossed out of that building like trash
in that one instant my whole reality changed. I went from a
caged five to a broken zero with no place in the society I lived in.
Someone from the high council informed me of this personally
when my compensation was doubled. He conducted the trans-
action at my hospital bedside with no consideration given for
the injuries I was still suffering from.' She paused and took a
long drink of the tea.

'I came home. At first I shut the world out but I found it a lonely
existence. I felt empty. Lost even. One day I walked past an alley and found a baby thrown out with the rubbish. After making
inquiries with the help of the high council I refitted my house for
rescuing the lost, the hurt and for those who have nowhere to
go. The girls are the children no one wanted but me.'

She took a breath and sipped her tea before continuing, 'They
are all trained as fives and if they choose to contract themselves they go only to vetted contracts. Some choose to remain
with the ballet, some train in the fashion house, others work in

my office because they have a head for business and yet others still train in the kitchens. I went from losing one child to caring for many.

Then I found those who were broken hiding in the shadows of life. I had already set up the fourth level as a healing and wellness clinic. Everyone who comes here are inpatients and nobody is ever asked to pay money. The ones I can help leave with hope. There are those who prefer to stay here. They live in a females dormitory on the next floor up with the girls and will have a home for the rest of their life.' Mari could see that they were impressed.

She had taken a horrific situation and given many hope from it. She operated in the shadows because she took care of those no one else was willing to see. It was almost as if she had managed to create a thriving community within the wider one. A tribe of her own. 'Who will see to your people if you contract with us? Nick asked interested in the world she had managed to create for herself.

'I have a system in place that will allow me to keep on top of what is happening when I am not available. I will have to have access to a com device so I can deal with anything Jo cannot handle. This will create a need for me to have a couple of personal hours every day.' Maybe mainstream society had no need of what she did every day but those that did would suffer the most if her new system didn t work well. Mari was aware that getting things right had taken a lot of trial and error the first time around. She hoped it would not take as long for Mercy House to settle into running smoothly without her.

'What kind of modifications have you made in your personal quarters to cater for your...' Mari watched as Susanna floundered searching for the right words that would not sound offensive. She covered Susanna s faux pas smoothly with the words for her, 'My damaged leg. I have handles throughout my apartment. More specifically there s one beside the bed, the necessary and in the bathing room. I have a handle over the bed to help with getting up in the morning and I would need a dancers barre. I have my stick of course and comfortable seats throughout.' Mari appreciated the thoughtfulness behind the question. These would be the everyday little necessities she would need that almost no one ever took notice of. Maybe she was asking so the changes to her personal area could be made ahead of their arrival if she agreed to the pre contract

'How do you manage your medical care?' Nick asked and elaborated before Mari could reply, 'It is three days by horseback to the nearest town. We do not always have a healer available. We would need to pick up any supplies you will need before leaving the city.' Mari raised her eyebrows at the lack of healers in the territories. She had not been aware that things she had always taken for granted were sorely lacking elsewhere. 'I have some stretching exercises that seem to help if I do them regularly enough. If the pain is particularly bad I have to take a couple of extra pain pills through the day.'

Nick and Susanna seemed to be having another of their wordless conversations. Mari took a sip of her tea while she waited patiently for them to rejoin her. Even if they modified her rooms for her she had no idea if she could survive in the world they knew. She had no knowledge of the world outside of the dome city she had been born in.

The couple finished their unspoken conversation and Susanna rose to take her turn to serve fresh cups of hot tea. Mari lowered her leg to stretch the muscles. She left her stick beside her chair and limped to the sideboard for a piece of fruit. She offered the plate to both Nick and Susanna. Susanna chose a segment of an orange and asked, 'Do you eat a special diet?' Mari laughed then explained, 'Everyone inside a dome city relies on the package dehydrated stuff and then substitutes that with whatever fresh food they can get their hands on. I had to learn how to cook so that I could learn to make what I was eating edible but that was long before the hotel existed in the building.'

As she reseated herself Nick asked, 'Can you defend yourself should the need arise?' The smile slipped from Mari's face and her grey eyes turned cold, 'Yes. Do you need a demonstration?' She watched through narrowed eyes as he placed his fingers together and regarded her over the top of them. She was not sure where his line of questioning was leading.

'Everyone needs to be able to defend themselves in the territories. It is a wild place. Some people are not satisfied with what they have and come looking for what they can take. There have been times when we have had to fight to keep our land and our way of life.' Nick was straight with her. Mari relaxed marginally. He had had his reasons for asking about her skills. 'What is your preferred weapon of choice?' He asked sounding curious.

Mari picked up her stick and pressed a hidden button. She removed a wicked looking knife from the top. 'Stick and blade. Although I am proficient in other weaponry as well.' Nick's eyebrows raised, 'What if your assailant brought a gun? ' It wasnt as if this thought hadnt crossed her mind before. Mari smiled as if butter wouldnt melt in her mouth, 'They do not need to know that I wear bulletproof garments as underwear now do they? The weapons I am showing you right now are not the only ones I am carrying.'

'How does your leg affect your fighting?' Susanna asked. Mari knew question wasnt relevant to the negotiations. Mari had had to work hard at perfecting her stance and she expected the Jacksons not to believe her answer but it was all she had to offer them. She contemplated their expressions as she spoke calmly, 'It doesnt. Good fighting technique is about balance and stance not brute force.'

Mari returned her blade to her stick. She had never revealed her abilities to anyone. It had been the first new skillset she had trained for after the healers had deemed her fit enough. She had tried to work with her innate abilities although her skills with weaponry had progressed much faster and it was these she usually relied upon when faced with a nasty situation out in the rim tenements.

'We will hear you now.' Mari noticed that Susanna looked relieved that the knife had been concealed again. She had not seemed comfortable talking weapons. Mari picked up the notebook she had been writing her questions in earlier that day. 'You must forgive some of these questions. Mercy House has a vetting process that we usually follow for all potential contracts and there was not much I could cover in such a short period.' She had not been able to detect anything about the couple other than they had arrived in Spark City over three weeks ago. Her contacts had told her they were staying at the Enterprise Hotel on the outer edges of the inner city and that they had been watching her for about four days.

She watched as Susanna touched Nick's arm preventing him from asking the question he had been about to. They were now only able to speak freely in answer to a question she was asking. Mari looked down at her notebook examining her neat list of questions, 'How did you come to the decision to approach me with the contract?' She looked up as Susanna answered, 'We heard whispers of a five so exquisite that no man could afford her contract price. We heard she used a stick but nobody knew why. We heard she rescued babies from dustbins. She took home the injured and abused. We kept hearing stories of the woman known to many as Lady Mercy. We followed the stories.' Nick took Susanna's hand as he added, 'This was after we saw you barefoot in the park.'

Mari knew that there had to be more to the truth than what she had just been told. She covered her movements so well that not even Jo knew all her secrets. Mari's information network had let her know that she was not the first female they had approached. The others had ended negotiations. The information dossier stated being asked to leave the safety of the city as the sole reason. She needed to hear the couple out. They had come a long way. Something felt a little off about the whole pre contract ceremony to her.

Lowering her eyes to her notebook Mari spoke decisively, 'You have not spoken much of your son Scott. It is irregular for him to be missing from this ritual. What kind of a male is he? Has he agreed for you to act as his proxy?' Rare curiosity reared its head giving way to intrigue and an intense craving to know more about him. Their body language told her that they had been hiding something. The look they had exchanged with each other told her that it had something to do with Scott. Pain and hope. Two very powerful emotions at war with each other. On their faces. In her heart.

Susanna answered softly, 'Scott is 33. He does not believe in the idea of the contract. Anna's laws are not the only way to live in the territories and he is conflicted about whether they are the best way for him. A little over four seasons ago he lost someone he was planning to mate in horrific circumstances. You will find that he is an enigma but he has a good heart and is capable of loving deeply once he is willing to accept you.'

So one choice was already mated and was offering for her to be a third in a triad. Her other choice would be a challenge to deal with while he was getting used to the idea of a contract. Mari could understand Scott's pain. She didn t like that Susanna had not answered whether or not that he knew they had approached her on his behalf. 'How do you make a living?' She winced internally knowing how rude the question usually was in polite circles. Having seen enough underhanded fraudulent business dealings in the city and the blatant misuse of females in the rim tenements this had become one of her standard questions.

'We come by our money honestly. I farm the same piece of land that all the previous generations of Jacksons have as far back as before the time of great unrest. Most years are good ones but we have years when the cities add to the technology we use to harvest with. Those years can be rough.' Nick answered. Mari instantly followed up with, 'What is it that you farm?' Nick smiled. She could see that this was a subject he held close to his heart. 'We farm geothermal, solar and wind energy and send it to the energy banks for the cities to draw from.' He stopped at the look on her face and added, Anything you don t understand we can explain to you as we travel. If you are willing to join us.' Mari knew the basic concepts behind the old technologies he had mentioned but made a mental note to ask more about them anyway. She mentally ticked down her list and realized she had come to logistics and supplies. 'If I agree to the pre contract period what will I need to bring that is not readily available where you live?'

'You will need everything but will have little use for couture formal wear. Colors that blend into the landscape, fabrics that wear well as we only travel to the city to shop once a year. Good shoes and your personal items. Try to limit baggage to three trunks and a travel bag.' Susanna answered with a smile. She too had once asked that same question of Nick and his brother.

'If I choose to leave the city how many days total will we be travelling for?' Mari knew that the cities were all connected by trains but didn t know how long it took to get from one to another. 'We will be travelling for five days in total. Two by train and three by horse drawn wagon.' Susanna answered and anticipated her next question, 'We need to leave the day after tomorrow in order to beat the storm season and still have time to do one last trip to Bordertown for supplies before we get snow bound.'

There was a storm season? Mari raised her eyebrows at this piece of news. Inside the dome the weather was kept on a regular cycle. On good days the dome was lowered and on others it was raised and the bio system kicked in to keep the weather nice. Even the stars on some nights were fake or so she had heard. She did not know what snow was.

She was aware that she had asked all of her questions. She knew that she would never forgive herself if she let her one chance to regain some semblance of the life she had once led walk out the door. Her real concern however was Scott. She had a feeling that they were attempting to contract with her more for their son than for themselves. Mari sat in quiet con-

templation for a few more minutes before raising her head.'If
I agree to contract with you there will be no caging unless it
is necessary to save lives.' She spoke with conviction as she
added the ritual words that would signify the end of the negotiations, 'We have heard each other. I am prepared to face this
choice and will sign the pre contract for a 30-day period after
which the contract will be also signed by the chosen male. Do
we proceed?' She waited for their answer about caging.

'We do not believe a female should be hidden from life. It will
be as you have asked. Only if your life is in danger will we ask
you to lock yourself in a small space and wait.' Nick answered
matching her conviction and Mari nodded her thanks. She
opened the folder that had sat on the side table during the entire meeting and removed the paperwork that would be required
for the initial signing. She placed it on the low table between
them.

'We want to read through the contract if that is acceptable to
you.' Susanna phrased her request in such a lovely manner that
Mari didn t have the heart to tell her that with the exceptions
of the points they had already discussed of the safety clause,
her need for personal time, modifications to her quarters and
caging it was still a standard contract. Mari picked up the
paperwork and handed it to her. She stood and picked up her
stick,' I will be outside in the hall. Please let me know when
you are ready to continue.' She draped her head wrap over her
hair and refastened it before making her way slowly out of the
room. Time passed slowly as she stretched her leg by pacing
the length of the hallway. On her third turn she noticed the door
had opened and Susanna was waiting for her.

When they were seated again Mari asked, 'Are you satisfied with
the contract?' Susanna smiled at her, 'You have been more than
generous with us.' Nick asked seriously, 'Are you sure about
this? You seem to have made your decision without hearing us
today.'

She had facilitated more than her fair share of contracts for

Mercy House. 'I would have had you both removed if I was un-satisfied by anything I heard and this contract would never have-seen the light of day. You are worried that Scott will not accept the actions you are undertaking on his behalf. I am not entirely comfortable that he isnt here and I accept that my decision will be binding him into a situation he may not be ready for. Is there anything you wish to add to the contract?'

'No. Scott will have more terms to add before the contract peri-od begins.' Susanna answered as she signed on behalf of her family and watched as Mari signed her full name without flour-ish. They repeated the paperwork in triplicate and she reminded the Jacksons that the master copy would be filed with the High Council as it was the requirements of Spark City. As she placed the paperwork to one side she asked, 'Would you like a full tour of Mercy House now?'

Chapter Five - Scott

He felt tormented daily by the thought of life without her. Numbness was the second skin that had clung to him with tenacity for the last four years. Nothing made sense without his Rachael. At the thought of her he winced internally. The man he had become without her was someone she would not have recognised. She would have passed by him without a second look. He had obtained an icy hard shell that helped him keep it all together.

Underneath it, he still felt like his insides were being shredded by razor blades. His mouth hardened into a straight line. He was not going to allow himself to get sucked under by the wave of emotion that was threatening to engulf him. He had to learn to deal with the fact that she was gone without losing sense of himself and his surroundings. His Rachael had been the most beautiful thing about his life. She had been his ray of sunshine able to lift his moods on the blackest of days. She had captivated his attention entirely and after four years he was still struggling with the fact that she had been ripped away from him so cruelly.

Scott blamed himself. Her death had been the horrific result of a trade gone wrong. He had thought that he would be giving her the news she had been waiting for that they would finally have a home of their own. Instead her mother had been waiting for him. Her dress had been covered in her daughter's blood. The grief had been etched deep in her face.

He hadn't waited for goodbyes. His father had taken over his responsibilities and placed the torch to the pyre that would carry his beautiful female to the next world. Scott had watched from the very edge of the forest. Camouflaged so that no one would know he was there. He couldn t bear to say goodbye to her then and he still wasn t sure that he could.

Scott knew he had wandered the territories for about three years. He had lived off the land and stayed in travellers caves. When he came back to himself he had been sitting on the edge of a cliff eating an apple without a care in the world. As soon as he had been able to gain his bearings he had worked his way back to Bordertown and from there-home to the farm.

Scott had been whittling a piece of wood aimlessly one evening when Susanna had realised he had a real talent for carving wood. Their home was now full of added decorative elements that made it unique. It made him feel as if he hadn t been away for all those years and as if he belonged even more.

Susanna had encouraged him to work on an even larger scale. She had turned over the guest suite of rooms and allowed him free reign. Only two days ago she had sent him a list of things that needed to be added to his masterpiece without an explanation why.

He stood in the finished room in the dark. A bottle of bourbon loosely clasped in one hand. He had a very bad feeling that they had had hidden motives for their trip to the city. Lately Nick had been getting restless. He had been arguing with Scott a lot more and urging him to move forward with his life.

He had suggested trying a contract as a way of something differ-ent. Scott had disagreed. Loudly. How could he move on as if Rachael had never been? How could he sign his name to a document that elevated females no higher than glorified breeders.

He hoped that his gut feeling was wrong but it was screaming that everything was about to change again and he didn't know if he was ready.

The next afternoon Mari leant against the wagon watching the farmhands mill around Susanna and Nick. She wished to give the family space to greet each other properly after their time apart. She had been in awe of the wide open spaces outside of the city. Every day sounds that Susanna and Nick had told her was quite normal had overwhelmed her at first. Everything had been muted inside the dome city. There were so many new things she had been experiencing every day. It was as if she had been wrapped up inside a blanket her entire life. The world was so much more beautiful than she had been led to believe.

Every morning before they had eaten Mari had let Nick test the extent of her training. He had not been joking about taking her training further. She had not exaggerated her skills with her stick and knife. He had finally been satisfied that she could handle herself when she had bested him twice with her knife resting against his carotid artery. He had dusted himself off and introduced her to the crossbow. His reasoning had been that she would not always have the weapons of her choice close to hand. Even Susanna had shown her how to hold a rifle and aim for a moving target. She had turned out to be quite the markswoman.

Mari brought herself back to the present and observed Scott's interaction with his parents while she was able to. He seemed to be warm and genuinely pleased to see them. Susanna had warned her that he would change as soon as he discovered her true purpose for being present. Mari thought that he must take after his contract mother in looks. He had piercing green eyes and dark hair grown slightly too long by city standards. She shook herself mentally. She was not normally so judgemental about someone's looks. Mari braced herself beneath her travelling robe as his gaze turned her way.

Scott strode across the dirt yard toward her. Mari forced herself to hold her ground. He was as big as Nick and just as intimidating. The top of her head barely reached his shoulders. She watched warily as he stopped just in front of her blocking her view of the mated couple she had spent the best part of a week learning to trust. His eyes darkened slightly and he spoke to Nick and Susanna as he circled her. 'Who is this? A damaged domestic?' Mari refused to flinch or move a muscle despite the fact that he was purposely crowding her space. 'Where did you find her? Bordertown?'

She could see no evidence of mating marks. He moved with the easy grace of a big predator. Underneath her loose robe she moved into a fighting stance. If he was more unstable than his parents knew she would be ready to defend herself. 'Honey, you d be better off in the city where they can take care of you.' Mari knew that he would not be able to see any of her features as the deep hood of her travelling robe had been chosen for that purpose alone.

'No. 'Mari spoke in a calm voice interrupting him. He stopped moving for a moment and contemplated her before he removed her hood to reveal her simple lavender braid and silver eyes. She watched as the happiness drained from his eyes and a cold look settled over his features. She looked ahead as he circled her again then half turned so she could see Susanna's determined face. His stance stiffened some more and as he turned to face her she could see the betrayed look she had expected.

His face held a lost look on it before he collected himself and sneered, 'Well isn't this an interesting colour. A city girl... really Susanna? You had me refit the house for a useless...' Mari's hand shot out from underneath her robe and covered his mouth. 'Maybe you would like to rethink your next words. I suggest you don't say them.' She did not flinch at the anger in his furious eyes,' My name is Marianna...Mari to people who like me. It's a pleasure to finally meet you.' Keeping her gaze steady on his face she cautiously removed her hand.

'You don't like Strangers-I get that.' Mari looked at Nick who was edging his way closer without making the situation worse. He gave her a nod to keep talking, 'My pre contract was not signed by you. I think you will find I am far from useless no matter where I have come from.' She continued to meet his furious green eyes. When she spoke again her tone was more conciliatory, 'I am happy for you to discuss my presence and all the issues surrounding it. I will leave you in peace right now if you would please point the way to a necessary. I will remain out of the way until someone comes for me.'

Diplomacy had become a way of life. She was not going to say something she could later regret. She watched as he gave her a grudging nod. Mari could feel herself swaying slightly on her feet and knew that there were shadows under her eyes as the pain in her leg had reached intense levels.

'Your rooms are last on the left off the corridor.' Scott pointed at her luggage, 'Don t get too settled if I have my way you will be returning to the city as soon as possible.' Mari wordlessly picked up her small sling bag. It contained a change of clothes and everything she would need straight away. She looped it across her body and made her way inside the ranch style house without another word to the two men. Susanna attempted to touch her arm briefly as Mari passed her.

The minute her back was turned the loud voices erupted. She could hear a lot of anger and pain in their voices. 'We raised you better than that. You owe her an apology.' Nick sounded furious. 'You brought her here! You know why I didn t want a contract! She s little better off than a slave to our needs and desires. What about Susanna? Did you think about how this will make your own mate feel?' The absolute fury combined with deep hurt made her pause in the doorway, 'Why would you do this?' She thought she heard that lost note in his voice again.

Mari could hear Nick's low rumble as he began to answer his son. Scott's words sounded worn. The argument must have been a longstanding one and she hoped that one of them would concede before the situation deteriorated into physical blows.

She could hear Susanna's voice trying to soothe them both as the door shut behind her. As she looked around the room she quickly located the central corridor and turned left as directed. Scott had more of a point than either Nick or Susanna realized- Mari mused as she swept aside the curtain that had been left hanging in place of a door. Her last contract had used to treat her as exactly that, a beautiful high priced slave who had only been put on the planet to please his every whim.

As her gaze swept around the room she gave a small sound of complete delight. The whole room had been clad in wood paneling that had been carved into. The walls resembled a garden with mountains and a flowing stream. On the fireplace mantle were matching flowers and the bed head was a work of art within itself.

She had a small sitting room with two chairs with foot rests grouped in front of the fire place. Beside one of them was a lamp for reading. She continued through the large archway again. She had not noticed the work space in the corner with a large hand carved desk and a com. She had extra chairs and handles where she had requested them to be. Mari followed the room around and found the necessary in the bathing room just beyond a walk through closet area.

Mari took advantage of the facilities and returned to the sitting area leaving her small bag in the bedroom. As she came through the archway she noticed Scott waiting for her in one of the chairs. He had a knife out and was shaving one of the flowers in the mantle reshaping it until it was just right. He seemed lost in his work. She stopped and waited until he noticed that she had joined him not willing to get any closer while he had a weapon in his hands.

'They told me.' His voice was cold, hard and flat. 'What did they tell you?' Mari stayed where she was. She had witnessed a betrayal out in the yard and knew that she had been told about it before she had signed. He was obviously struggling to be civil to her.

She found herself observing him from under her lashes. He was vulnerable and hurting for reasons that were not hers to know. He spoke again the tone of his voice had not changed, 'What they did to find you. Who you are and what you do where you come from.'

'What else did they tell you?' Mari kept her voice as neutral as possible. He stood up and turned to face her, 'I standby what I said. I know you heard me.' She looked at the floor as she answered, 'I heard you. Contracts screw up lives in ways you can't possibly begin to imagine.' His anger was beating at her and she felt drained. She knew he didn't really understand her world or the many layers of captivity she had existed in.

'Why didn't you have them thrown out?' His eyes were as cold as ice and she involuntarily shivered. 'Because the laws state that I must hear them out once the ritual words are said.' She added softly, 'I had no choice.' He came closer, 'There is always a choice. You made yours when you signed.' She stood absolutely still. She still felt like he was a predator barely leashed. Nick she trusted. She still felt unsure of his son.

'Dinner is in one hour,' he gave her grey dress the once over, 'wear something more complimentary.' 'I will need my luggage.' She stated softly as he tipped her face up so he could see her eyes. He stood waiting until she glanced into his eyes voluntarily. She found no comfort from the conflicting emotion swirling around inside of them. A small furrow appeared on his forehead. 'You are not afraid of me.' He studied her face for a few more seconds before adding, 'Just unsure of how I will act. Your luggage will be brought to your rooms. Leave the formal city be-

havior outside this room. This is your private space to be yourself.'

Scott could see her thoughts rapidly chasing over her face. She
was making a visible effort to keep meeting his eyes. He could
feel her body trembling and he backed off half a pace. Mari
spoke finally, 'Did you have a chance to read the contract?' His
face tightened. He had briefly scanned the contents of the document. He had had to have Susanna explain exactly what 'caging'
meant.

'Is there anything you wished to add immediately?' She wanted
to know so she would not break any boundary lines straight
away. Scott's expression did not change as he absorbed the fact
that she was asking for his preferences. 'I will tell you those if
any at a later time. Dress in something pretty.' He finally answered.

Chapter Six - Help me to understand

Dress in something pretty. Mari unpacked one of her new dresses. Jo had chosen them on her behalf as she had an exceptional eye when it came to clothing. The dress she had pulled out was a deep violet colour that showed tantalising flashes of skin whenever she moved. She brushed out her hair then braided it back into one thick rope hanging down the centre of her back.

She put on a matching amethyst choker and earring set before sliding the de Montmercy ring onto her right index finger. She looked in the mirror before deeming herself ready. Scott had wanted the butterfly. She hoped he wouldnt crush her wings.

Maybe it wasn't wise to pit father against son straight away but she only had 24 days left in which to choose which male she would contract with or the consequences could be serious for all involved. The high council saw breaches of contracts as personal attacks on the laws of Anna. The sooner she could extricate herself from their grasp the less stressful her life would be.

Mari's stick tapped beside her softly as she arrived in the dining area. She took her time to examine the soft furnishings and craned her head up at the vaulted ceiling. 'Nick's fifth forefather built this house with his bare hands. 'Susanna was already seated at the table dressed in a mid-green dress for dinner, 'Are you alright?' Mari took the glass of wine she offered and nodded. 'I feel out of place. Uncertain.' She admitted softly, 'You were right when you said Scott is an enigma.' She watched as Susanna sipped her wine thoughtfully then spoke the words, 'You have not had time to find your feet yet. Give Scott time. This will not be easy on anyone involved until he accepts that this choice is happening. His father fought it as well. You will need to expect everything in this choosing. Nick will not make it easy for Scott. They will say things to each other in the heat of the moment and may take liberties with you in front of each other.'

Susanna reached across the table and gently squeezed Mari's hand, 'It was so at my choosing between Nick and his brother. Just be yourself and don't play their games.' Mari took the seat opposite Susanna at the table. 'Please forgive me but at what point do I tell them that I am not a live doll to be torn in half for their pleasure?'

Nick leaned down beside her and took her stick from her hands. She watched as he placed it in the corner way across the room from her. She had had no intention of drawing her knife if she felt threatened. She watched warily as Scott sat in the chair next to her. 'We will stop when you have chosen.' Nick sat in his customary spot beside Susanna as he signalled to the kitchen staff that they were ready to be served.

Mari sat motionless as she was served a fresh salad made up of things she could not identify. 'I thought this would be easier on your stomach.' Susanna said softly and pointed at each item as she spoke, 'Lettuce, tomatoes, cucumber, onions, mushrooms and avocado. On the centre platter are various types of dressings and cheeses.' She imitated Susannas motions with the knife and fork before softly saying, 'Thank you. I did not recognise any of these.'

'They do not know what food looks like in the city?' Scott asked his parents and as Mari's skin turned an interesting shade of pink she answered for them, 'Fresh fruit and vegetables are shipped in from outside to substitute a dehydrated meal. They are not always readily available so everyone has a supplemental drink through the day to help keep healthy.'

She let the conversation ebb and flow around her as she continued to eat her meal. As she took a sip of her wine she met Nick's eyes across the table then turned to find Scott staring at her. She arched an eyebrow at Susanna, 'Did I miss something or have they just found the secret of my dress?' They shared a conspiratorial laugh.

Scott had woken early the next morning as he often did. His rooms were across the corridor from Mari's and he could hear the soft cries of pain from there. He had initially just gone to check that she was alright but had ended up staying to watch over her. Her deep sleep had been punctuated with agony and he wondered what had been done to her to make her so afraid of males.

He must have made a noise because she turned her head as she stretched under the covers. Her silver eyes widened with confusion but to her credit she only asked him calmly, 'Am I late?' He watched as she reached up for the grab handle he had installed a few days ago. He focused on the floor while she began the undignified process of getting out of bed. When she had stopped moving Scott assumed it was safe to look up again.

He had spent most of the night tossing and turning over the words his father had said. He had been right. He owed Mari more than the anger he had displayed for most of the previous day. It was not her fault that he used it to cover how broken he was inside. 'No.' He replied as he handed the glass of juice from beside his chair to her. She placed it on top of the bedside table between them and found two pain pills from a container in the top drawer. As she studied the glass he spoke again, 'It's juice squeezed from an orange. People drink it for breakfast. '

'Thank you, I know what an orange is. ' He could hear no sarcasm in her voice only her gentle statement. 'You are not to blame for the anger I displayed yesterday.' Scott watched as she settled back against her pillows. She sipped the juice again. 'It is still early. Did you need to see and hear the reasons behind the renovations?' he could detect no condemnation in her voice still only confusion but it had been mixed with a note of pain.

He found that he had slightly furrowed his forehead and as he relaxed it he spoke the formal words Susanna had told him to say if he wanted to hear her story, 'I would have nothing but truth between us.' His poor attempt to keep her customs tugged a small smile on her lips. 'You were crying in your sleep. You were in pain every time you moved. Will you tell me why?' He phrased his request less formally when she didn t speak he added, 'Help me to understand.'

Scott watched her break eye contact with him as she picked out a spot to stare at on the wall in front of her. He guessed that it was a heavy subject for her to discuss first thing in the morning but knew that he could not take back the words now even if he wanted to.

'You were right when you said I had made my choice. I signed the document because I felt trapped in the life I was living in the city.' She began tentatively before taking another tiny sip of the juice,'I had exchanged the cage of my first contract for a silken one created by the high council. One I was suffering in. My truth makes people angry, uncomfortable, embarrassed and upset. Many say that what happened to me should never have been allowed. There was no one to shield me from it. I have seen your anger already and this is not an easy subject for me especially first thing in the morning.'

Scott swallowed. He had heard part of the story from Susanna the night before. He squared his shoulders. He was able to handle whatever she had to tell him but she was right he had displayed a lot of anger around her and his intimidation had obviously had an adverse effect on her. 'I was furious but it was not you who caused it. I will control myself.' He took note of her white face as she quickly braided her mass of hair over one shoulder to keep it out of the way.

She nodded silently before opening her mouth to begin again. 'You have asked me for my truth when all I have seen of you is cold fury at a situation that is not of your making. ' She straightened her shoulders as she spoke, 'You want me to trust that you will not hurt me.' He watched as she dug deep within for the courage to keep going. When she looked up he was startled that her silver eyes met his green ones, 'I told you that the contract screws up lives in ways you cant possibly begin to imagine. I m taking a chance on this one. All I have heard from both you and Nick are words. Words are easy. Your actions will say much more to me.'

'What are you so afraid of us doing to you?' Scott's words were gentle. She looked terrified. He watched as she pushed the bed covers down to reveal her legs below the hemline of her night gown. He leaned forward and picked up the soft throw at the end of the bed. He handed it to her and watched as she draped it around herself. Her hands were shaking slightly as she showed him her bad leg. It was misshapen with a long ugly scar down the center. Large bruises ranging in various shades from blue through to yellow covered it and as she reached forward for the covers he helped her with them.

'The bruises are mostly from travelling so hard and fast to get back here.' She explained not meeting his eyes again. Scott waited for her to collect herself and when she did she began to speak, 'In the city males use Anna's laws as a legal way to abuse their females. I believe that I paid the price for something my mother has done. She trapped me in her contract by an illegal clause called the freedom clause. She substituted my freedom for hers without my knowledge or real consent. She drugged me and guided my hand as I signed what I thought was the keys to my new apartment. I was caged and broken to do another's bidding without question at all times and when her contract tired of playing with me he kicked me off a third story balcony. My unborn daughter was lost. I died. The healers forced me back into the shell lying on the table below me.' She turned so he could see the scars on her back peeking out of her warm wrap.

Scott felt his mouth harden into a flat line. He knew that his eyes were chips of emerald ice in his tanned face. He was glad that she continued without looking at him. 'After I had healed, males attempted to take liberties with me that they would normally have had to contract with me for. This happened more than once. I went to the high council and brokered a deal. The high council could surround me with as much security as they liked, I would pay them whatever money they asked for and they would let me set up a refuge in my family home so that I could offer hope to the those living without it in Spark City. I had begun to see the others that society only saw as invisible. They needed the same help I did and no one but me seemed to care. My home became Mercy House.'

Scott had watched her as she kept speaking to him. The pain stamped all over her body spoke to him in ways words hadn't. He noticed her peeking up at him through her eyelashes. He remained silent battling the all-consuming anger that seemed to be his constant companion. He was waiting for her to tell him as much as she could before he spoke again. The look on her face begged him to believe her words, 'When I signed the pre contract with your parents I had a lot to consider. Many other females could lose what sense of peace they had finally found. In the end my decision hinged upon just one thing. I could con-tinue to live for others and disappear into the shadows myself or I could take a chance on a new contract so that I could start living again.'

He was lost in thought as she slid out of bed and limped towards the bathing room for a few private moments. He knew he must have made her feel naked to her very soul and he wondered how long it had been since anyone had seen that much of her. How long since she had truly given all of herself into someone else's care without knowing that there would be no recriminations. He guessed that she was dressing so he made the bed for her and went to stand before the picture window framing the mountains in the distance.

When he had designed this room he had been sharing the beauty of what he had seen with Rachael. Rachael was already at peace. Mari sounded as if she had yet to find her's. Maybe her staying in it would help her too. Scott had noticed that she had put some of her belongings around the room making it more of her own than his. There were colors of muted greens and blues everywhere. He heard her sit in the chair he had just left. 'The girls you find. Do they contract?' he asked suddenly. 'If they choose to.' Mari replied softly and added,'I make sure that the family is well investigated before negotiating on behalf of anyone in my care.'

He turned so that she could see the raw anger on his face, 'What happened to your contract?' He had his emotions well contained and hoped he was not scaring her. He was outraged that she had had to go through such atrocities. He watched as she swallowed, 'I have heard conflicting stories. He was sentenced to death for murdering my mother after he left me bleeding on the pavement. I have heard that he was sent to the territories and I have heard that the high council had him hanged. I dont know which to believe but I like to think that he is dead so that no female will be hurt by his hands again.'

Scott watched as she folded her hands in her lap waiting for his reaction. 'It is different here.' He said tightly wishing he could be more reassuring, 'No one will harm you like that again.' He strode across the room and disappeared through the heavier curtain she had hung across the door the previous night. Her quiet statement of 'I hope so' reached his ears as he disappeared behind it.

He needed space to think and the only place he had been able to do that lately was in the work sheds. He heard his father joining him as he tinkered with part of a wind turbine in an attempt to get it functioning again. 'She wants to believe he's dead.' He said without looking up. Scott could hear his father sitting on one of the crates they used of storage beside him. He stilled his hands as he looked up at him, 'When were you going to tell her?'

'Tell her what?' His father was giving him the space he needed to work through the reaction he was having to her past. He bowed his head to look at the wind turbine again, 'The high councils send the scum of the cities out here to plague us. They do not do their own dirty work. For all we know the bastard's roaming near us.'

'Susanna thought exactly the same thing and that's why she insisted that Mari be covered at all times when shes not on the farm. You thought she was just a domestic yesterday before you removed her hood. Mari is every bit as deadly as she looks delicate. She has a warrior's courage and a kittens heart.

She has what it takes to survive the territories if we let her find her way.' His father sounded as if he had chosen his words carefully. Scott's hands paused as his green eyes met his father's blue ones, 'It may not be enough. Im going to ride the boundaries and check the defenses. It will give me time to process this and her time to settle in.' 'We protect what's ours.' His father stated calmly. 'We protect what's ours.' Scott echoed the Jackson family motto back at him.

Chapter Seven - The Territories

'Do you have time for me to show you something?' Mari looked up from the report she was reading to find Scott standing in front of her. She had not seen him in the house or around the farm for nearly a week. She looked down at the papers in front of her again.

'Finish your work. I can wait.' He moved in to her sitting area and folded his tall frame into one of her reading chairs. Mari concentrated on the work in front of her again. Her decisions were all made from the reports that were being fed to her. She had to get them right or the impact would be bad for those she had come to care about. The reports were starting to flood in from Mercy House faster than she was able to keep up with them.

'I missed spending time with you these last few days.' Mari spoke between reports looking up to find him watching her. 'I was busy reinforcing the farm boundaries and defenses.' He replied and commented, 'You're working too hard. Should I ask Susanna to strike a better balance for you between your contribution to the farm and your work with Mercy House?' She scribbled a note on the pad beside her and put the report she had just picked up down on top of it.

'This can wait.' She said quietly. She tucked a stray hair back into her braid self-consciously. She had known that he would need time to process her story but she hadn't expected him disappear entirely. As he turned back toward her she rose then sat right back down. She absentmindedly rubbed her bad leg. Scott looked over at her. Mari hoped he hadn't caught the two tears of frustration that rolled down her cheeks unbidden.

He stood before her with her stick in his hands. He put it down leaning against the wall beside her as he crouched down to meet her eyes. 'Will you spend some time with me?' He reiterated. A confused look flitted across her face as her fingers brushed a matching head covering and he nodded. She hid all traces of her hair then reached for the hand he offered her. He offered her his elbow for her to thread her hand through and as she rested her hand on his arm he picked up her stick again with his other hand.

He led her out into the night. Out into his large private garden to the relaxed outdoor setting under the trees where they could both see the stars. Mari took a deep breath appreciating the thought that had gone into this moment. She could see candles and blankets. What looked like an antique ritual tea set sat ready to be used on a table under a branch. Scott took a blanket off the end of the couch and settled it around her shoulders before guiding her into a well-padded chair with a foot rest.

'Truth telling time.' He said pouring her a mug of tea. 'I have given you the truth of me.' Mari spoke before she sipped her tea. In the night air her tiredness was starting to subside. 'My truth.' He sat opposite her his face half wreathed in shadows, Will you hear me?'

He hoped she would. He had spent his time away dealing with the cause of the anger that had made her so wary of him. He wondered if he was doing right by everyone involved by continuing the contract ritual like Susanna suggested. She had advised him that he needed to help Mari understand the truth of him and why he had reacted badly during their first meeting. She had travelled so far from the safe home she had created. He had seen hope in her face that day when she had put him in his place.

Mari looked up at the stars. He was giving her another side to consider should she choose him. Everybody had a story and she had not heard his yet. She knew he was watching her as she sipped her tea stargazing. Her facial features settled into the familiar serene expression as she replied, 'I will hear you.' She rested the mug of tea on the low table between them then folded her hands on top of the blanket and waited.

'You will have heard that there was another in my life for a very long time.' If he closed his eyes he could still see her hair ha-loed in the sunset of a late summer's day, 'Rachael was fire and laughter to me. We met in school.' At her confused look Scott added,'It's a place that people in the territories send their children for training in numbers, spelling, writing and history. It runs if there is a learned person in the area willing to take on the role for a time.'

He waited for her to indicate her understanding before continu-ing, 'We met every time my family had to go into Bordertown for supplies. After a while we decided that we were moving beyond a simple friendship into something so much more. Our families met together for a meal and an understanding was reached. In the city you call it contracting. Out here we call it courting. We were courting for a long time and saving up to buy our own piece of land. We alternated our time between the farm and Bordertown.'

He could still feel the horror of the news that had greeted him when he got into town. She had died because someone had felt he had taken advantage of them in a trade. They had gone after him by hitting his only soft spot. 'Her mother found her murdered out behind the necessary. Someone had cut her up pretty badly. When they told me she was dead I died inside too. I saddled my horse and rode away. They tell me I wandered for years before I came back to Bordertown and from there back to here.' Scott took a breath and a couple of gulps of tea, 'I was merely existing until the day you showed up and told me to mind my manners in not so many words.'

All the thinking he had done while he was out mending fences had been leading up to this moment. He watched her from deep within the shadows that he was sitting in. Her expressive face held no judgement for him for losing himself. Her face only showed distress at his loss and pain.

'I didn t come here to replace your memory of someone you obviously loved deeply.' Her voice was troubled as she accepted more tea. She watched as he added something out of a hip flask into his. 'Susanna explained that you were not told much about me in the city.' It had grown cold and he grabbed another blanket to add to the one he had already wrapped her in.

The candles were burning low and he fingered her head covering as he crouched down beside her. He kept his voice as gentle as he could, 'I hate the idea of any contract because you are worth more than a piece of paper and an arrangement. My father had his reasons for what he did. He was right when he told me I have to move on and make room in my life for someone who is alive.'

He ran his hands through his hair, 'Do you think you can be patient with me? This may take some time to adjust to.' Mari knew he was giving her a glimpse of who he had once been. She tried to meet him half way in his thought process, 'I can do that. Will you hear me further?'

He sat in the chair beside her as she struggled with the words. 'I've already woken you in the night with my nightmares. You are asking me to be patient with you. I need the same from you in return. I do not recognize a lot of the foods that have been placed in front of me this week. I feel too exposed whenever I go outside. We are both in a place that requires some finesse.' When she finally spoke she could see that her words had made sense to him. 'Tell me what you need me to add to that piece of paper.' He said in a low voice, 'You asked me if I had any extra terms after we first met and I do.'

He reached over and removed her head wrap gently. He watched as she folded it neatly. 'I don t want you to cover your hair again. You re not just a nameless female now. You mean something to this family. You will still have to wear your head covering outside of the boundaries. If we contract, we will contract to court with a view to mate.'

At her confused look Scott explained further, 'Here we court and then mate. What I m proposing is that we change from the city way of doing things to the one that makes sense where we're living.' Mari waited quietly sensing that she needed to hear everything he had to say. 'You will be treated as a cherished equal.' He took her hand as he asked, 'Is this agreeable to you?' He had not embellished his formal wishes with pretty words but the meaning behind them left her speechless.

No one had ever seen her as anything but a contracted female, a slave and an invisible. Somehow he had begun to see something in her that she did not recognise within herself. As she sat thinking his offer through and examining everything he had said she was aware that time was passing by. Scott prompted her 'Mari?'

The emotions were still flickering over her face faster than he could read them. 'It is more than I ever dared hope for. You have thought those terms through?' She asked still trying to grasp the magnitude of what he was offering her.

'Yes.' He was fully aware of what he had just done. She was not Rachael but he believed his parents had found a treasure worth his time. Deep down he knew that he would be on edge every time they left the compound until he had seen her fighting skills for himself. 'I like your terms.' She said softly looking up at the stars.

'I'm glad you came.' his statement startled her slightly. She couldn't see his face in the dark. She heard him striking a match before he lit the wick in an oil lantern. His features had rearranged themselves so that he was smiling. 'The laughter is slowly returning to this house. Dad is more settled and Susanna has another female about the place.'

'Has she no daughters of her own?' the words spilled out of her mouth before she had a chance to reign in her thoughts. Scotts voice sounded ominous as he replied, 'She had one. We haven't heard from her since she was given permission to visit for their mating. She was younger than me by ten years. Liana had only been in training for three years.' Mari quickly did the math. Susanna's child would be a young female of 21. 'They try to visit each city at least once every dry season. Susanna hasn't given up hope that her daughter is alive and the mystery of how she disappeared from the train will be solved.' Scott took a swig straight out of his hip flask.

Words escaped her for the moment. His family had survived so much sadness. 'What do you miss most since leaving the city?' The question was so left field that Mari laughed for the first time in his presence. She thought for a moment before answering, 'You wouldn't believe me even if I tried to explain.' He raised an eyebrow as he waited.

'I miss my cat. I had a cat who would come to my window some nights when I was lonely or sad. Eventually we began to trust each other and he began to appear for regular attention.' Mari shook her head and smiled, 'When he snored he almost sounded human.'

A few days later Mari was seated at her desk and opening her last report of the day as Scott entered her sitting area. He watched as the papers slipped through her fingers. Her expression was one of horror as she whispered, 'It cant be true.' The colour had drained from her face as with shaking hands she picked up the paperwork only to make an agonised noise of denial.

Scott was beside her in a few short strides. He took the papers from her hands and read the news for himself. A man had gotten past the hotel security and scared her personal assistant. His description given to the guards when they arrived had matched one John Smythe.

The same John Smythe who had been banished for her attempted murder and the murder of her mother Elanna. Jo promised she didn't give out any information of her current contract but since they had footage of him in the office she couldn't be sure that he hadn't dumped a copy of their files onto a portable drive.

'They told me he was dead.' Her eyes were swirling with the hurt the news had brought her. She was making a real effort to keep it together in front of him and he noticed she had an unshakeable grip on her stick. 'They also told you they had released him to the territories.' Scott reminded her in a hard voice, 'The dead have their permission to rise if they can survive five years out here in the wilderness.'

'It's a pretty safe bet that he's survived then.' Her voice changed slightly as she contemplated what her next move should be to protect Mercy House from unwanted cyber attacks. 'John Smythe.' She looked up at him. 'He was the male who...' her voice trailed off at the evident fury on his face. Scott made a visible effort to calm himself down before he scared her. He put the papers on her desk in front of her. 'He will not get near you again.' He promised.

Mari rose and placed her hand on the side of his face. She waited until his green eyes met her own. 'I may have a healthy amount of terror of this male but I can defend myself if necessary. I will not take any risks. ' She waited until he covered her hand with one of his own, 'See that you don't.'

Mari watched the anger at her pain and the fury of his helplessness in the situation burn in his eyes. His grip on her hand tightened slightly. Already he was sliding back to that dark place where he had lived for far too long after he had lost Rachael.

'Scott.' she spoke softly hoping to get through to him, 'I'm still here. Right in front of you.'

He was displaying some of the symptoms for being in a catatonic state. He was unresponsive, his stance was rigid and he had stopped meeting her eyes. She had had females in the rehab rooms that had similar conditions that had been brought about by a prior traumatic event. She thought that he could still hear her even though he wasn't responding to her words.

Mari guessed that he was dealing with a sudden influx of bad memories that threatened to keep him trapped in the past. 'Scott!' This time she was more forceful, 'I'm alive. I'm not Rachael!' She read his face. His hand tightened painfully on her's. His blank stare told her that he was still fighting those memories.

Her fear for her personal safety had passed and now she could truly see why Susanna had been terrified for her family. Scott must have turned into a walking shell. She tried one more time, 'Scott! Get out of your head. If you stay trapped in your past this life will pass you by. I will pass you by.' Mari lowered her gaze thoughtfully.

He blinked. Good. He had heard her then. She would not need to use a physical prompt. As he shook his head to clear his thoughts she felt his hand loosen right up. 'Mari?' He searched her face. He knew that he'd just frozen at the mere threat of her life being hurt. 'Are you going to freeze if I need your help?' She asked calmly as she took a step back from him allowing him room to breathe.

'I'm not her.' She reminded him gently as she waited for him to collect himself. Eventually he rubbed a hand down over his face as he answered, 'I know.' 'How long have you been freezing?' She asked softly. 'Whenever the memories get too bad.' He admitted and turned to the window ashamed that she had seen him lose himself over a possible threat.

'I can help you if you'll let me.' Nick stood framed in the door

way. He felt as if he were witnessing a miracle. Mari had managed to get Scott to open up more in the past two weeks then
he and Susanna had in nearly three years. 'I'd appreciate
it.' Scott turned and looked at his father. An unreadable look
passed between them containing volumes of a conversation.

Mari quietly returned to her desk leaving them to start the
healing process. 'I'll meet you in the turbine shed in twenty
minutes.' Nick flicked his eyes to the woman waiting almost motionless in the corner, 'I need to speak with her.' Scott nodded.
He raised a hand in her general direction as he left not trusting
himself to speak after showing her how weak he felt he was.

Nick looked at her, 'Thanks doesn't quite cover what just happened does it?' Mari raised her eyes and replied gently, 'It
isn't needed. What is important is that he's ready to talk to you
about what has been taking him away from you both. Maybe
he will start to train with you again.' He watched as she flexed
her hand a couple of times and then stacked her papers neatly.
'Were you thinking of offering your healing services out here?'
He asked and as she nodded he added, You've chosen a hell of
a place to do that in then. Susanna asked me to find you. She
is waiting for you in the living area.'

Chapter Eight - Bordertown

Bordertown reminded Mari of the frontier towns she had learned about in her history classes. As they had rolled into town she had noticed that there was only one main dirt street in the centre of the town with double story clapboard houses and storefronts to either side.

There was only one hotel and it was situated as a combined business with the bar. The haphazardly built fence surrounding the town only had a front gate a back gate and the train arches which had automatic sliding doors at either end.

Susanna had told her that the town's latest innovations had been the wooden sidewalks and street lighting. They had made the trip to pick up the last of the supplies they would need before the long storm season set in. What used to be known as winter could stretch as long as six months outside the dome cities and it was not wise to travel far from home if you did not want to freeze to death.

They had been in town for two days. Mari and Susanna had just finished up at the grocery store and were feeling happy with themselves. Their morning's trading had gone well. Mari had watched as Susanna had haggled with the owner to exchange 3 large crates of fresh fruit and vegetables for staple rations and medical supplies.

They had decided that it would be safer for her to masquerade as Susanna's new domestic. Mari was concealed beneath her earth coloured cloak and everyone had been treating her as if she were invisible again. It was refreshing to be able to watch people without being expected to interact with them.

She followed half a step behind Susanna as was the custom for a domestic in the city who was accompanying their mistress. She was enjoying the slow bustle of being in town and learning all the best places to shop. Mari knew they were heading to-wards the parcel office next to collect the shipments that were awaiting them there when without warning someone bumped into her from behind.

She felt Susanna's hands steadying her until she indicated she had regained her balance by a quick nod of her head. Her hood was obscuring her view to either side of her head. She listened as Susanna asked whoever had run into her, 'Are you alright? My domestic is not trained properly yet.'

'It was my fault entirely.' Inwardly Mari gasped at the smooth tones. She sneaked a peek at him as she turned to face Su-sanna with a worried look on her face. He had the same self assured smirk on his face that he always displayed to females that he wanted to impress. Mari lowered her head in a pretense of shame as she rapidly sorted through all their options.

'Would you allow me to buy you a drink later this evening as an apology? I m sure my mate would not like for me have caused you any offense.' Susanna spoke again and watched as he ignored her altogether. He reached out and ripped off Mari's hood painfully. 'What are you doing all the way out here in the territories little Marianna?' When she did not reply straight away he continued, 'Did you think I wouldn't recognize you with this on?'

She resisted the urge to rub at her head where strands of hair had been ripped out. He pointed to the very faint scar at the base of wrist. 'I branded you there one night and in defiance you cut my ownership mark right off with your dinner knife. I had to put in five stitches to stop the bleeding.' Mari knew she needed to get Susanna off the street and away from John. He would not have paid attention to anything she had said after offering to buy him a drink.

She brought her stick closer to the front of her body as if readjusting her balance and turned her body so that Susanna was half shielded from him. 'John.' She greeted him coolly as she moved so that Susanna was fully shielded behind her body. Her whole focus had narrowed down to him. She could not afford to let her emotions rule her. 'Protecting others as usual,' He observed, 'Defiant to the last arent you.'

'Something is clearly wrong with you. You didn't own me then and you don't own me now.' Her voice came out surprisingly strong.   'Of course I do.' Johns hand moved like a blur and grabbed her arm in a painful grasp, 'Elanna gave you to me.' She attempted to pull herself free of his grip. She replied calmly, 'Elanna drugged me and gift wrapped me for you without my consent. I am not going anywhere with you. Susanna would you please go get my chosen. Hurry.'

She refused to let her eyes leave his as they silently waited. She could only imagine the psychotic thoughts running through his mind. She took a silent cleansing breath before facing him unflinching of his obvious scorn. 'You are a defective female who never did know her place.' John attempted to shake her as he attempted to drag her from the street into a small alley. Mari had been prepared for the moment he would attempt to yank her off balance. She rolled the motion through her body and continued standing her ground.

'She knows her place.' Scott seemingly materialized out of nowhere to lean on a post beside her. She shook her head slightly at him as he surveyed the scene in front of him.   He had watched her continue to hold her ground against the much larger male. He was surprised that she was managing to hold herself under such iron control. He pulled his knife out from the holder attached to his belt and leisurely began to clean his fingernails with it.

'She is far from defective. ' He watched as his father appeared in the mouth of the alley with a gun casually trained on John from their other side. His father's usual warm demeanor had turned menacing. He smiled an ice cold smile of his own and John started. With two of them flanking her they presented John with a united front. He watched as Mari took the opportunity to try and extricate Susanna from the altercation by sending her after the parcels they had waiting at the parcel office.

He was pleased that she had remembered Nick's warning that Susanna was no good in a close quarters fight. Susanna looked at Nick for guidance and he nodded once. They all wanted her at a distance with her gun trained on their target. Her sharp shooting was the best back up plan they had if it came to a fight. As Susanna slowly backed away Mari spoke again to distract the male who had her in his clutches, 'I suggest you remove your hand slowly and walk away John.'

A small cry of pain escaped from her as John twisted her arm in his grasp even more painfully. She knew he had never taken suggestions from others well. Mari could recall many times he had walked into her room covered in the blood of some hapless fool who had tried to tell him what to do inside his own house. She hoped that this moment would not end in blood as well. 'Elanna said that to me once.' Mari could read the hurt in his eyes. Her mother had walked away from them both and never looked back once. Mari spoke softly, 'Elanna liked to play games with people. I'm not her. Please let me go.' She could see out of the corner of her eyes that Scott was circling around behind her moving backwards from post to post slowly. Nick had drawn back a bit to give her room to move should she need to fight her way free.

'Call your men off Marianna.' John bit out. Whatever plan they had forming she hoped they would act swiftly. She allowed him to see a small smile then, 'Why? Are you afraid that I might actually walk from you this time? Both my men have you dead to sights but they're not the ones you should be afraid of.' She caught the quizzical look Scott flicked at Nick out of the corner of her eye. She knew that Susanna would have them covered from the parcel office.

Mari adjusted her grip on her stick with her thumb covering the button that would release her knife. John raised an eyebrow at her, 'Surely not the delectable female you were shielding from me.' They were attracting too much attention. A crowd was gathering on the opposite sidewalk on the other side of the dusty road.

'Susanna is only one of your concerns. Just let me go John. You are accomplishing nothing with this.' Her silver eyes met his dark ones without reservations. She had stopped being afraid of him a very long time ago. The only fear she had in that moment was how badly he could hurt the people she was coming to care deeply for. 'You are mine Marianna.' He laughed bitterly at them, 'Alive or dead. Do you think your friend has better manners? '

Susanna had just returned with her arms piled high with parcels. Mari could see the round muzzle of her handgun strategically placed at chest height in between the parcels. Nick stepped in front of Susanna and Mari could feel Scott at her back. 'I would not wish you upon any female.' Mari breathed in through her nose and exhaled through her mouth silently. He was truly trying her patience.

'Enough.' Scott spoke directly in her ear, 'Break his grip and then leave. He will not listen to anything you say.' Mari was comforted by his closeness. She eyed John warily as he swung his attention back to her, 'You will need to give me room.' She felt his warmth leave her as she moved quickly twirling her stick up only to bring it down with all her strength hard on top of John's hand. He dropped her arm and before he could reach for her with his other hand both Nick and Scott shoved her behind them. They stepped in front of her hiding her from John's view.

'Go back to the hotel and wait for us.' Scott spoke not taking his eyes off the furious male in front of him. He felt Susanna's hand on his tense shoulder like a silent promise that she would make sure they arrived back to the room safely without further incident.

He felt as if he had ice flowing his veins. He had had to watch Mari stand her ground and calmly converse with the male who had once killed her. She had put her own pain and terror aside to make sure Susanna had been safe before she had acted.

They closed in on John backing him up against the wall of the nearest building. Scott's hand was itching to teach the male a lesson he would never forget. He had a feeling that in her own quiet way Mari had already done that. From everything she had told him John was a male more used to having females obey his every whim. Her act of aggression against him would keep him emotionally off balance. 'Get them packed.' His father said his tone solid. Scott knew better than to argue when he heard it. He slid into the long shadows that had begun to swing their way in the early afternoon sun after shooting John one last dark look full of promise.

Nick shot a feral look at the scum who had dared to accost the females of his family in public. He had been keeping his eye on John Smythe long before he had gone to the city. He knew things the male wanted to keep hidden. He knew things that would affect the balance of their entire society. 'We've got business to discuss.' Nick watched John cradle his damaged hand. He was proud of Mari. She hadn't backed down from the person she had feared the most in the world.

'I know all your secrets.' The male looked at him like a cornered rat and Nick continued knowing he was making a lethal enemy, 'You were the one my son traded with for land four years ago. If he had remembered who you were he would have carved out your heart for murdering Rachael Saint. That female did not deserve the death you gave her. The only thing you need to re-member is we protect what is ours. Marianna is most definitely ours and we don't take kindly to any threats to our females.'

'You won't see me coming.' John sneered. Nick eyed him with distaste. 'I won't have to. Stay away from us.' He buried his fist deep in the male's stomach for emphasis before leaving him crumpled on the sidewalk.

Chapter Nine - Rebekah

She could hear them speaking to her through the fog that surrounded her. 'Honey.' Susanna pressed a drink in the hands that she couldn t stop from shaking. Her face swam into her view. Concerned. 'Scott. I think she's becoming unresponsive.' Susanna's face seemed worried. Inside her head Mari was screaming in agony. 'Leave her be Susanna.' Scott hadn't moved from the window where he had been keeping watch on the situation below. Mari wondered vaguely what was happening outside.

She wished she could reassure Susanna that she was alright. Susanna had been hovering ever since she had collapsed into the chair nursing her arm. John had only been toying with them. She knew his moods intimately. He had definitely been interested in Susanna. The intense pain in her arm was beginning to cut through the fog surrounding her thoughts.

A movement at the window drew her attention. Scott had turned to face them. His face looked as if it could have been carved in stone. She shrank into the chair. Her control had slipped enough that her face was a transparent shade of white. Scott swiftly crossed the room to stand in front of her.

They didn't have the time for her to lose her courage. Scott noticed that her hands had finally stopped shaking. He crouched down in front of her and spoke gently, 'He hurt your arm. I need to see how badly injured it is.' The family would need to move fast once his father returned if they were going to make it out of Bordertown completely intact.

Mari had had her hair exposed for far too long and many had noticed. So many that he had been watching a mob gathering some distance away and begin their descent down the hill to the hotel. 'I need to see.' He repeated softly and took her hand. She focused on the floor with a troubled expression on her face. Scott pushed her sleeve up and examined it thoroughly. She would have one hell of a nasty bruise. 'We had eyes on you the entire time.' He kept talking to her calmly, 'Susanna I need a bandage.'

He waited until Susanna had handed him the bandage and he began speaking to her like she was a skittish horse, 'News travels fast here. All the unattached males know that there is a fifth in town. We need to get you out of here as fast as possible without detection.' Susanna placed her hand on Mari's shoulder and they both took note of how she jumped at the contact. 'Have you much unpacked.' He heard Susanna ask. She shook her head and swallowed hard.

Mari had not expected John to change in all the time he had been out of her life. He hadn't. She had thought that she would have been much stronger inside if she ever had to face him again. It had felt for most of the exchange that her heart had been trying to pound through her chest.   'He still scares me. ' She volunteered the words just as Scott was checking that he hadn't wrapped her arm too tightly.

'Why couldnt I stop shaking?' words continued to fall from her lips as if the dam she had been holding inside herself had finally burst. She sounded broken. Vulnerable. Mari hated feeling this way. Tears were threatening to spill at any moment but she knew that there was no time for her to fall apart.

'It was the adrenaline leaving your body.' Scott knew she need to be distracted or she would fall apart despite the impressive performance she had put on in the street. 'How long have you been training?' He asked moving his tall frame to sit in the chair beside her. He watched her close her eyes briefly before looking up at him, 'Over eight years.' She hadn t deliberately hidden the fact.

He had seen her full training sessions every morning on the way to Bordertown and that was only with her knives. He had a feeling that his father had wanted her to keep her staff fighting techniques a secret just in case she needed to use them in an attack at the farm. Scott still had no idea what she was really capable of and he was slightly curious to see what else she could do. 'Time is running out. You may have to choose with no notice.' He was concerned that she had not had enough time to make her decision, 'Are you ready for that?'

Mari dipped her head slightly in acknowledgement. She had made her decision over the course of the last four days. Both males were worthy of her spending time with them. She just didn't know how to break the news to them. 'Are you?' she asked softly in reply. Mari watched as Scott tucked in the loose end of the bandage.

Without answering he squeezed her good hand gently before moving back to the window to keep watch. The crowd had grown larger during the short period he had been tending to her. With his back turned he let the fury he was still feeling cross his face.

In the next room Nick eyed the crowd gathering under their windows with a grim face. Susanna joined him. 'A head covering isn't going to work to get her out of here.' 'Can you hold them off for at least an hour?' She asked him. She had an idea but it would take time to develop. Scott stood in the doorway with Mari just behind him. She looked at her mate, 'I can disguise her but I need time.'

Mari looked in the mirror not knowing what she expected to see. She certainly didn't look like herself anymore. Gone was her hair colour. Susanna had dyed it a deep brunette. She had bought the bottle at the grocery store as an insurance policy and it had been needed straight away. Susanna had not stopped trying to reassure her that she would see her own hair colour return in no time at all but it was still a huge shock to see a stranger staring out of her reflection back at her.

Mari inserted the blue colored contact lenses she had used in the city as part of her costume for Lady Mercy and sighed softly. Susanna had convinced her that her hair could be a liability during a close quarters fight and without any more explanation had cut it back to her waist. It certainly made holding her head up lighter but definitely threw her balance off.

Dressed in a deep blue tunic over matching leggings she no longer resembled herself at all. She wasn't sure how she felt about so many needed changes within one day. Susanna tucked a stray hair into the single braid falling down the center of her back before they walked in silence back to the room that their males were standing guard from.   Mari had signed into the hotel as Susanna's missing daughter Liana from Oceania City when they had first arrived. She supposed Susanna had attempted to give her her daughter's coloring as well. Nick circled around her with a critical eye and as she waited for his opinion Mari noticed Scott was resting his hand on the butt of his gun.

Scott heard his father say, 'I think the disguise will hold.' 'Her bandage and her limp.' He noticed John Smythe moving through gathering of overeager males. He was moving quickly from one to another whispering their ears. He had no doubts that he was giving each one of them a description of her right down to the scar on her hand. Scott knew in order to smuggle her out the devil would be in the fine details. He doubted they had enough time left to get a head start on the crowd before they started their rampage.

He turned as Mari was receiving a jacket from Susanna. He watched as she draped it over her damaged arm and walked steadily without a limp from one end of the room to the other.

When she turned to face them she asked, 'Convincing enough?'
'Not me.' Scott pointed to the window, 'Them. Convince them if
their alcohol soaked brains haven't already started seeing you
in every shadow. We have to go before they bust down the doors
and break in here.'

'Need a hand with your escape?' a female stood in the doorway.
She wore a red cloak with a deep hood. The unknown female
pushed her hood back as she urged. 'You need leave with me
right now. Times wasting. They're already in the building.'
Scott made the introductions as they left the suite, 'Mari this is
Rebekah. Rachael's mother.'

Mari knew he had not laid eyes on the female since the day
she had discovered her daughter's body. She listened quietly
as Rebekah quickly explained that she would hide them at her
house while Nick and Susanna took their wagon to the caves.
She assured the older couple that she would personally drive
them out to the caves once it was completely dark. 'How did
you get into the hotel?' Susanna asked her friend. Rebekah
pointed down as she answered, 'The tunnels. Scott showed us
how to navigate them in case there was ever trouble.' Mari took
the hand Scott offered her as she squeezed Susanna's hand
silently in farewell. She almost missed Nick and Scott exchange
long looks before they split up.

Rebekah led them through the maze and right up into her kitch-
en through a trapdoor. Scott slid the wood box over the top of it
hiding it from sight. He knew that he owed her an explanation
for the way he had acted but all he felt was an overwhelming
sense of shame. They had both lost someone precious to them
and instead taking responsibility he had run away.

'Rebekah, I...' He begun knowing there were no words to explain
the enormity of how he had been feeling when he had left. 'You
have nothing to be ashamed of.'Her voice cut across his as she
removed her hood, 'I heard the stories. I know you ve suffered.
We'll talk about it when you arent being hunted by a pack of
fools.' She took a set of keys off a hidden hook on the wall as

she continued, 'Its good to see you... son.'   Her piercing gaze lit upon him again, 'You can spend the day in the storm cellar. I knew that drifter would cause trouble no end when I first laid eyes on him.'

He turned to Mari to make the proper introductions, 'Marianna de Montmercy meet Bordertown's Elder-Rebekah Saint. Rebekah is family.' Scott watched as Rebekah enveloped Mari in a hug. 'You're the cause of all this mess then. Don t worry. You're in good hands with this one. I wish you'd kept the purple hair though made a real change from all the brunettes walking past the window.'

Mari flicked her eyes at Scott shooting him a helpless look and he shrugged a silent *just go with it* back at her. She gave Rebekah her full attention as she said, 'I didn t come to town to cause a riot. We needed the supplies and John is an old contract who does not like the word no.' 'I surmised that when you cracked him over the hand with your stick.' Rebekah waved at the windows in the next room, 'Got myself a prime watching position there.'

She watched as the female turned to lead the way through the house. They stopped only once for a quilt against the damp and a basket of food. Scott realized what she was about to do and removed a rug before opening a trapdoor with a lock. 'The lock's new.' He commented. Mari took the quilt and supplies so that Rebekah could unlock it for them. 'Never know who I have to smuggle out of town.' She thought the other female was being deadly serious as she lifted the door.

Scott lit a lantern that was sitting on a hall table. As he descended first the lantern cast out a soft light to reveal the room below. He took a quick look around the small room. Nothing had changed. There was a couple of armchairs, a bed and a wall of storm season supplies. He watched as Mari made her way down the narrow stairs carefully. Her eyes had grown large as she realized that they would be locked in the small space. He spotted the moment her thoughts returned to her memories of caging. He pulled her close as Rebekah began shutting the door above them, I'll be back at sundown.'

'Be safe.' He reminded her. As he looked down at Mari he caught a tear sliding down her face unbidden. He watched as she stepped out of his embrace and sat down in the chair. She removed the contacts that had made her eyes a deep blue and stored them in a pouch on her belt. Scott picked up the quilt and draped it around her.

Mari pulled it around herself more tightly and bowed her head. John had returned. Her emotions had begun to overwhelm her. 'Hey.' She looked up to find Scott's face close to hers, 'We ll get through this.' He reached forward and fingered the end of her braid, 'Your hair will grow back.' Before she could re-gain her control another tear slid down her face and he caught it on the end of his finger.

He moved swiftly and picked her up with a hand under her knees. Scott eased back into the chair she had been occupying with Mari cradled in his arms. He sat motionless waiting for her to speak. The shirt under her face was growing wetter and after five minutes she raised her tear stained face to look at him, 'What if he finds us here?' Scott tightened his arm around her as he spoke, 'We will deal with whatever and whoever comes our way.' He pressed her head back against his chest. He liked the feeling of having her resting there. 'Sleep. There's about six hours until sundown.'

Scott held her through her nightmares and whimpers of pain. He had not thought that Rebekah would welcome him back with open arms especially with a potential courtship in tow. He looked down at Mari, she had known him for such a short time and he wondered where her thoughts had been leading her.

He knew that compared to his father he would be a fool to think she would choose him. He had nothing to call his own other than what he had managed to put away towards a piece of land. His father had a successful energy harvesting business.

He had already made his plans to leave when she chose against him. It was just that way things had always been done in the territories. The thought hit him like a sledgehammer. He was beginning to care for Mari as if she was his own. He leaned his head back on the top of the chair as he explored the errant thought further.

Opening her eyes slowly she was hoping against hope everything they had been through had just been another one of her reoccurring nightmares. She scanned her surroundings and sat up slowly aware that Scott had his hand in her hair. 'It was not just a nightmare then?' Her heart felt heavy as she slid off his lap and limped around the room to stretch her cramped leg muscles out. 'No.' he replied moving the lantern closer to them making the little circle of light engulfing them slightly brighter.

She dug in the food basket and offered him an apple. She waited until he accepted the piece of fruit before she spoke again, 'I don't think I could have handled being in here without you. ' He stilled as she continued, 'You asked me earlier if I was prepared to cut this choosing short and I am.' She looked down as she poured two cups of coffee from a thermos. When she looked up she felt bad at the disappointment written clearly on his face. 'You don't think you have a chance?' she asked softly as she handed him his cup.

'Why would I?' Scott retorted. His tone softened as he explained, 'I have nothing to offer you. Dad has a business, the farm, money and you would have Susanna to help you get used to living in the territories. ' He took a mouthful of the coffee as he watched her move back toward him unsteadily and take a seat on the edge of the bed beside him.

'I chose you.' She finally said as she realized he was waiting for her to tell him otherwise, 'How could I not when you offered me so much more than I have ever had?' She had chosen Scott the night he had told her his truth. He had offered her a place in life that she had never dreamt could be hers.

Scott was struggling to speak. Susanna had told him the ritual words for accepting a contract but he couldn't say them. They didn't feel right to him. 'I am honored.' Was the best that he could manage. She had turned her head away from him and he knew she was giving him the space he needed. 'Mari.' He spoke in her ear.

She turned her head so their eyes met. He had moved silently from the chair and kissed her forehead. Scott had appreciated her giving him a minute to process the magnitude of what had just happened. Her eyes were huge and he wanted to see her smile again, 'What other weapons can you use?' He watched as she smothered a laugh. Her face finally settling on a familiar half smile.

'I also use a knife.' She reached over and grasped her stick, 'See.' She pressed the hidden button and withdrew it. Scott took the knife from her and tested the sharpness of the blade. He watched as she hid the knife and placed the stick back against the bed. 'In all honesty,' she began with a small smile, 'stick and knife are just the beginning. I like to tinker with weaponry.' Mari took compassion on him and asked into the silence 'What is a cave?'

 'A cave is a natural formation in the rock causing connecting room sized hollowed out areas.' He answered factually having observed Susanna explaining nature to her in this way. 'We use them to hide when we need to leave town in a hurry.'

Chapter Ten - Escape

The trapdoor creaked open and Rebekah stood outlined in the opening. Her gaze transferred from Scott to Mari and back again as she said in a low voice, 'I knew you would be good for him from the minute I laid eyes on you.' She stepped back a few steps as they began to ascend out of the cellar. 'They're still hunting for you. Starting to go door to door searching by force. I've never seen the males in this town in such a frenzy over a female before.' She gave them the bad news as she tossed one of her spare cloaks at Mari who caught it one handed.

It was the trademark red colour of an Elder. Mari knew that there would be major repercussions for her if Rebekah was caught harboring them within her home. The consequences would be even more severe if one of the high councils heard she had given away one of her badges of office. Scott took the cloak from her hand, shook it out and began fastening it at her neck. She knew he would make sure no part of her was showing when he reminded her, 'Don t take risks.'

She raised her face to his and countered, 'If it comes to a fight remember not too get too close. I trust you to guard my back. There s no one else I want there. ' Mari watched him nod hoping that he understood that she didn't want him to shield her from the tough things in life but trusted him to guard her vulnerable spot. She could hold her own in a fight and knew he had not seen what kind of damage she was capable of yet.

Rebekah cleared her throat to gain their attention. They looked up and swiftly joined her in the dark back room. Only one candle was burning so that she could conceal she was not alone. 'The caves are not an option. Both the roads in and out of town are being watched. I can't keep you here in the storm cellar so I bought you train tickets to Spark City. I put it about that it's a planned trip to visit my sister there.' They exchanged worried looks but let her continue, 'Marianna is going to walk through town and board the train normally, Scott is going to use the tunnels and come up through the grate in the male's neces-sary near the platform.'

Mari thought quickly as they moved back through Rebekah's home and as they entered the kitchen she tapped Scott's shoul-der to get his attention. She undid the neck fastening as she mentioned, 'John recognized me by the scar on my hand alone.' They could hear the escalating roar of the crowd as it came closer.

'We need to switch places. Rebekah will guide me through the tunnels to you.' Mari handed Scott the cloak and took the pack the older female was holding. When he nodded she knew that nothing more needed to be said. He swirled the cloak around himself then took one more long look at them. She watched as he picked up the bag Rebekah had left at his feet and disap-peared out into the night.

The two females travelled the tunnels in silence each preferring the company of her own thoughts. Mari kept her mind firmly focused on moving swiftly without overbalancing or losing her way. She was also listening for the sounds that would indicate they were being followed. When Rebekah stopped ahead of her by a ladder Mari stopped and waited. The older female's brown eyes were serious, 'He cares for you. I know my Rachael would have liked you and wanted him to be happy.' She took something out of her waist pouch and handed it to her. It was a pair of glasses. The frames were out dated. 'Tell him to wear those. They're from my Simeon's days on the stage. Don t you forget those contacts either.'

Both their heads snapped up as the trapdoor above them opened and Scott dropped the cloak down to Mari. She put it back on without a word of protest. 'I'll get word to the caves tonight. Go quick and be safe. When this is over come and chop an old lady some firewood.' Rebekah told Scott as she disappeared into the shadows. 'Thank you.' Mari called after her into the darkness in a low voice as she climbed out of into the light.

Scott took her bandaged arm and lightly probed it checking her pain levels. He watched as Mari gritted her teeth against the pain he was causing her. He let go of her arm and they disguised themselves once more. As she settled into the deep hood of the cloak he warned her, 'They're already out there. You'll have to stow your stick and fake it onto the train.'

Scott snapped a wide cuff bracelet around the wrist of her uninjured arm. She looked at it and then raised an eyebrow at him silently. The bracelet was silver and turquoise. It was nothing like she had ever seen in the city. He briefly shook his head at her. They didn't have time to talk about it. He would explain later when they were safe. Moving swiftly to just beside the door Scott opened it a crack before opening it fully and motioning her to follow him.

He led her to the boarding office where they had their tickets scanned. The clerk commented politely, 'Elder Saint I didn't know you were planning to travel.' Mari remained silent and Scott replied on her behalf, 'Rebekah's sister in Spark City isn't doing so well. When she found out that I had to go to the city on behalf of my father's business it only made sense that we would travel together.' The clerk nodded politely and pointed out their carriage number to them before moving on to the next passenger.

They boarded the train without further incident and once they had settled into their suite Mari silently held her wrist up at Scott. While she had appreciated the gesture she was sure the bracelet served a dual purpose. 'I got you the bracelet this morning. Susanna managed to slip me a perception filter to put on you in case we ran into more trouble.' She watched as he touched the small blue chip that looked like a sapphire to her. 'You will need to keep it on unless you re under the shower.'

Scott had moved around behind the wet bar and poured himself a drink. Mari could smell the alcohol fumes in the air and without moving knew he had poured himself a well aged whiskey. She knew he was watching her as she ran her fingers over the fine work of the bracelet. He had chosen well. The blue stones went with the calm she tried to exhibit every day.

She watched Scott finish his whiskey before disappearing to examine the rest of the suite. Mari silently drew her knife and positioned herself in the chair in the corner of the room opposite the door. She pushed back the hood of her borrowed cloak and fingered the end of her braid missing the comforting weight of her usual length. When the train jolted she breathed an audible sigh of relief. She had half expected John or one of his men to have come crashing through the door in an attempt to stop them from leaving.

Scott returned to the living area in time to see her hiding her knife and feel the train pulling away from the station. He took a seat and asked bluntly, 'Where is your copy of the contract?' He hoped it wasn't back at the farm. The storm season was too close to arriving for them to return to Bordertown and then make another trip to the city again. 'My copy is in a safe at Mercy House.' She replied quietly. Mari didn't look comfortable at the prospect of staying in her former home. As if anticipating his next question, she added, 'I have another property where we can stay. Mercy House may not be entirely compromised but I can t be certain. I won't put anyone living there at risk if I can help it. ' 'He was on the administration level.' Scott reminded her. She looked down at the cuff encircling her wrist. 'He may have been on the administration level but not everything is stored there. My personal files and anything else related to me or my current location is being stored in a floor safe in the penthouse. It was sheer dumb luck that he found me at all.' Mari thought hard for a few moments before she added, 'The city is my home. We can disappear if we need to and not be seen for days. Nobody usually really sees me anyway. I'm an invisible.'

Scott realized she had always had a contingency plan because deep within she had always believed he would be coming back to kill her. She called herself an 'invisible' and in his world that word meant 'a nobody'. 'Don't say that again.' His voice sounded rough even to him, 'I see you just fine. You didn't like Susanna cutting your hair or changing its colour. You were scared to death of that bastard all the way through dealing with him but you didn't want him to hurt Susanna. You sing to yourself when you think no ones watching and you always revert to your city manners when you are unsure.'

Scott took a deep breath as she started unbraiding her hair. 'You're not comfortable with wide open spaces. I don't think you'd ever seen a live chook and I found you one afternoon curled up in the barn with the new kittens crying. I'm not sure about what though.' His voice softened, 'You make sure Susanna and Dad have the best food off the plates at dinner before you begin to help yourself. You have been showing more respect to them then I have in years.' He crossed the room and pushed her hair back from her face, 'I see you. I see you even when you hide behind your hair because you are uncomfortable. I see you even when you don't see yourself because I haven't been able to look away Mari. You've shown me who you are in a million little ways.'

Her emotions made her tempted to look away from the fierceness written across his face, instead she reached up and touched his hand, 'You have seen more of me than most have in a very long time.' He nodded and let go. Her heart was warm and she felt uncomfortable after all his revelations. 'You should know I sleep with a knife under my pillow.' she warned.

He grinned. 'That's okay. So do I.' Mari swallowed suddenly nervous. She felt as if he had seen through to her very soul. She knew she had chosen wisely. He gently took her hand and led her into the night area. Mari leant her stick up on one side of the bed. Scott picked up one of the packs and found what he was looking for quickly. He handed her a wad of material.

They had only been able to escape with the clothes on their backs. Scott was thankful that Rebekah was a thoughtful female who had found them both three changes of clothing plus what looked like all the appropriate accessories for Mari. He had recognized the dresses as previously belonging to Rachael. She was watching him silently with undisguised curiosity. Scott spoke gruffly, 'Go change. I'll keep watch.' When she had left the room he allowed himself to remember as his fingers brushed the soft fabric inside the pack. He upended it on the bed and rich fabrics spilled out in front of him. Too many memories assaulted him at once and he briefly closed his eyes before he began to put them away.

Mari returned still drying her hair with a towel just as he finished hanging the outfits up in the closet. Both packs lay empty on the floor beside him. He handed her a delicately embroidered wrap as she ran a finger over a particularly beautiful outfit. She had never seen anything like it. The fabric was silvery green in color and the embroidery was a delicate leaf and flower vine that wrapped around the hem of the skirt, neckline and waist. Interspersed in the throats of the flowers were delicate yellow pearl beads.

'Rebekah probably put that in there especially for you. You probably already have some fancy mating dress back at the farm.' She watched confused as Scott ran his hand through his hair. She shook her head silently in reply at a loss for words. Mating was a subject she had hoped they would approach once they had learnt to trust each other more. She replied softly, 'It has been a long day. I'll keep watch while you go and get clean.'

Mari waited until he nodded his agreement. She limped back

into the living area and took up his post by the entry door. She knew that there was no way she would be able to avoid talking about the subject if he raised it again. The door handle turned slowly and she held her breath. It jiggled a few times. The noise reverberated throughout the silent room. She heard a drunk female urge her male onwards realizing they had the wrong door. Mari gave thanks to all the ancient deities. 'Who was trying to get in?' Scott stood across the room dressed only in a towel with a gun gripped in his hands.

'Drunks.' She replied shortly as her gaze swept over his body. Her cheeks felt hot as she averted her gaze. She heard him leave the room. When Scott returned dressed in his loose sleeping clothes she was studying the electronic trip guide on the wall. It would keep them apprised of where they were and how long they had left until their stop.

'I'll sleep out here on the couch tonight.' He offered quietly when she finally turned around to look at him. The blush was still staining her cheeks an adorable shade of pink. She shook her head, 'The worst thing I will do is cry on you again. ' She laughed and added, 'Since that's already happened you might as well be comfortable.' Mari led the way back into the sleep area and curled up under the light blanket on one side of the bed. She knew the handle of her spare knife was sticking out slightly from under the pillow she had chosen while he had been in the cleaning room.

She patted the spare side of the bed with her hand. 'Are you sure?' he asked again leaning against the door. Mari real-ized that although she had contracted before he held the act of sharing a bed as sacred somehow. 'Did you and Rachael never share a bed in the courting stage?' She tactfully tried to put the question into his terminology. 'Of course but we had known each other for most of our lives.' Scott stretched out on top of the covers and rolled onto his side to look at her. 'This is a whole new concept to me.' Mari admitted feeling painfully embarrassed.

'Susanna talked to me about it some but she never covered what was and was not physically acceptable during the courting period.'

He lay on his back and put his hands under his head. He had never had to explain things before because everyone knew what to expect. 'In the city once a pre contract period is signed anything is permissible.' She stopped at his grim look, 'Did dad ever...' 'No.' She replied without hesitation. This was the awkward conversation she would have been having with Nick had she chosen the other way.

'Your way is one of respect and your father crossed no boundaries. Your traditions are important. I do not wish to be disrespectful of them.' Scott digested what she had to say and then rolled back to face her. 'You and I come from entirely different worlds.' When Mari opened her mouth to speak he held up a finger, 'It's not a bad thing. It just means we have to work harder at communication. When I talked about mating earlier you deflected the whole subject can you tell me why?'

'I know it's the ultimate sign of commitment between a contracted pair. I see women wearing their marks with pride. I was raised to be caged. My only outings were when I was bought out for important occasions to be shown off as an extremely rare and prized possession. Then I was hidden away from the world again. I have never owned a dress like the one hanging in the closet. It was not part of my training.' Mari hoped she didn't sound as ignorant as she felt.

Scott digested this new piece of information quickly. It made sense to him that she would be uninformed about the territory template. It fell to him to try to explain a mating ceremony to her the best way he knew how. 'A mating dress is an outfit made specially to show off your mate's marks. Each outfit is different because each male has a unique set of marks that he himself designs for his woman to wear for the rest of her life. You will wear the dress to the ceremony and then to every formal event after.' Scott added, 'Even the High Councils cannot refute mating marks. Rebekah knew what she was doing when she included it.'

He could see she was struggling with something and waited patiently. At length she spoke as if she was thinking aloud, 'The dress is really important then. Almost as important as the marks themselves. I don't want to seem disrespectful to your memory of Rachael by wearing her dress. ' Scott reached out and brushed strands of dark hair off her pale skin. 'Rachael was a large part of my life but that was a long time ago and she will always be a treasured memory. You,' His green eyes met her grey ones without reservation, 'need to stop worrying about hurting my feelings. Once the paperwork is completed and lodged no one has the power to challenge our choice.'

He waited until she had fallen asleep and then slipped out of the room quietly to watch the door. Scott nursed another small amount of whiskey he poured for himself. The incidents of that morning had changed everything for them both very quickly.

His private com signaled that he had a message and he retrieved it from where he had hidden it with a gun under a cushion in the chair in the far corner. Tapping at three keys in quick succession he opened the message and read it silently.

'Got your message. Do what you need to survive and to keep her safe. S. says listen to M. as the rules of her world are nothing like ours. Don't forget the weather is already starting to close in. D.'

Her world was infinitely more complicated than the lives his family chose to live out in the territories. He had listened to Susanna as she had attempted to educate them every time they made a trip to the cities. Scott checked his hidden weapons were still in position in the living quarters before settling down in a chair that he had deliberately angled to be diagonally opposite to the entry way.

Chapter Eleven - Making small talk

The next morning Mari dressed in one of the dresses she found hanging in the closet. Rachael had had exquisite taste in clothing. She could tell by the way the dresses had been designed and the fabrics that had been paired together. The suite Rebekah had booked them on the train was in first class so that they would only be disturbed by housekeeping once a day. She made a mental note to transfer the money back to her at the first available opportunity.

Mari checked the kitchen for food and found the cupboards completely stocked. She moved about on silent feet until she heard Scott moving in the sleeping area. He had not returned to the bedroom until the very early hours of the morning waking her as his weight sank down onto the mattress.

As she checked the electronic trip status on the wall she realized there was still another 24 hours in the journey before they would arrive in Spark City. Mari sat on a couch and tucked her bare feet up underneath her dress as much as she could. 'Morning beautiful.' Scott shoved a coffee pot under the machine and held up a mug as it filled, 'Want some?' He looked as if he had run both hands through his hair on his way into the living quarters. She hid a smile and accepted the cup he handed to her with a soft word of thanks. He drank his down in a few large gulps then refilled it. She drank hers slowly enjoying the flavor of good coffee freshly brewed.

'Have you used a com in the last twenty-four hours?' He asked into the comfortable silence they had created between them. 'Yesterday morning at the hotel while Susanna was disguising my hair.' Mari spoke calmly, 'I contacted Mercy House about a report and to let them know they could expect to see me in the building sometime soon. ' She had had no other choice despite the level of danger. It had been necessary for her to let Jo know the changes to her circumstances and that she would be in disguise on the arm of a companion.

Scott leaned back on the counter and eyed her over the rim of his cup. She was too smart to have said anything in her message that would give them away. He hoped John hadn't found copy of her codes in the files he had in his possession. 'There was no written copy of the phrase I used.' Mari guessed where his thoughts were heading, 'Nor is there any physical evidence at Mercy House linking me to my other apartment.' 'You definitely trust the person that you sent the message to?' He asked quietly. Mari nodded.

Joanna had been with her at Mercy House since she was twelve years old. She had trusted her with her life in the past and unless proven otherwise would continue to do so. If John had gotten inside Mercy House, then she really didn't know how many of her people she could trust. Her safe house location had always been a secret only she knew. Her sense of security had been stolen from her and despite helping others put their lives back together she had always had an errant *what if* in the back of her mind. 'You wanted a place to hide.' Scott guessed joining her on the couch. He couldn't tell what had caused the extremely lost look on her face a moment ago but he was relieved to see a sad smile appear.

'Amongst other things. I needed somewhere where I could be myself.' He watched as she put down her now empty cup slightly unfocussed and as she came back to herself she said quietly, 'The rules that I have to follow when I am in the city can be confining. I needed somewhere where I could breathe.'

Constricting rules ordered the daily lives for women. It was one of the biggest reasons Scott had never travelled to the city with Rachael. He hadn't wanted to put her through them considering she had grown up hidden in the territories in freedom. He wished he didn't need to ask her what they were but he had always lost interest when Susanna had reminded his Dad about blending into the background and pretending he knew what was expected at all times. 'Tell me what I need to know?' he requested knowing he would have to pay attention to what Mari would say.

She nodded. She had seen the flicker of disgust on his face when she had brought up the subject. 'From the moment we leave the train until we are in my apartment I'm required to walk half a pace behind you to show that you are my contracted male. I'm required to wear a head covering as only mated females may show their full head in public. I may only speak after I have been acknowledged by the dominant male in the room. You will know him as the most affluent male whom everyone is trying to please. If we are in a room full of women, I must seek permission of the highest ranking woman there usually a fifth to remove my head covering.'

Neither of them acknowledged the fact that even though she was a fifth she no longer had the hair colour to prove it. In fact, most of what she had said sounded like posturing for the alpha male and female to pay attention of those lower than themselves. It was a whole different culture for him and Mari took Scott's hand voluntarily. He looked down at their joined hands then up at her. She knew that he had never been out of the territories and had never experienced the type of societal claustrophobia that had been her whole world. She would have to come up with a more permanent solution for the way Mercy House would be run in the future. Mari doubted very much that trips to Spark City would be on their agenda after this one.

They spent much of the day in silence with Mari answering any questions Scott had about Spark City. Both were alert for anyone trying to break into the suite of rooms. Housekeeping had been by once to restock the food that they had eaten. As Mari cooked their dinner she hoped John had stayed behind in Bordertown but she knew deep within herself that he was not the type of man to give up on something he wanted that easily. The fact that nothing out of the ordinary had happened on the train so far had her slightly on edge.

'How long until your hair rinses out?' Scott had been quietly observing her from the doorway of the bedroom while she had been packing everything into their bags again. 'Susanna said forty-eight hours to a month.' She looked up at him. 'You are concerned?' He nodded. The city was someplace he had never been before. The customs were different and he had no idea of whether he could keep her safe as his family had insisted. She looked great as a brunette but he much preferred her with her original hair color.

'That's good.' at her words his head snapped up and as he looked directly into her eyes when she spoke again, 'The territories are dangerous in an outlaw old type town lifestyle. The city's danger usually lies within the politics and the words that people use. I don't have to tell you to trust your gut. I don't have to tell you that if they're coming at us with the intent to kill. Fight first. Talk later. Don't be disrespectful to any Elder wearing red no matter what attitude they take with you. I have seen you fight and I trust your judgement.'

Mari knew that the advice she had given Scott was against the law. Fight first-talk later could get a person exiled to the territories for the duration of a contract period. She just hoped that they would not be separated in the process. If they were caught fighting, their contract could be revoked and Mari placed in the training towers with all the female children as a house mother for the rest of her life.

She sat on the bed next to their bags. 'This is not going to be easy since John has spies everywhere. They're probably waiting for me to get off the train at Spark City. They may know by now that we are in disguise and exactly what to be looking for. They may not. Because I know the man so well I'm going to run with he knows and he knows where we are heading. If he wants to merely play with us he will use words in the high council to openly challenge your right to contract with me on the basis of inequality of equity.' She waited for him to digest the words *inequality of equity*. 'And if he doesn't want to play?' He asked seriously. Mari swallowed her face suddenly pale, 'John can challenge either of us for a fight to the death.'

Sanctioned cage fights over the access of a female was rare but precedent had been set in the past. Mari was sure John would know every law that he could use, bend and abuse to his will. Scott smiled grimly, 'I've seen you fight too. Dad and I have never seen anyone better at what you do with a stick and knife.' Nick had kept them all in training as they had approached Bordertown. She bowed her head for a minute in appreciation. 'I'm no cage fighter. He'd go for my leg first.' He crossed the room towards her. She peeked out at him from under her lashes. He had wanted to know what they were up against and once she had started talking she hadn't known how to stop.

She swallowed as he bent his head down to her level. 'If I didn't know any better I'd say you were being brave for my sake.' He was right and she gave a quick nod. He moved slowly and kissed her quickly. 'Don't.' He ran another hand through his hair, I know the odds and what we are dealing with now. Got me.' 'Scott,' He could hear something odd in her voice that stopped the next phrase from escaping his mouth. 'Yes?' She raised her eyes to his, 'Thank you for my first kiss.' He stilled and replayed her words through his head. How could no one have kissed her before now? He gave her a rare smile. 'There will be more. he promised in a low voice.

She picked up her sleeping clothes. 'Go have your shower.' He gave her the excuse she needed to escape the room. He retrieved his hidden com and sent his dad a quick message.

'Arriving tomorrow. No contact so far. M. holding up under pressure. Watch for us before the weather sets in entirely. S.'

Mari stood by the closet looking the outfit she had chosen to wear back into the city the following day over with a critical eye. Her hair color was just starting to wash out and she hoped that no one would challenge her to remove her head wrap. 'Are you alright?' Scott placed his travel bag beside hers. It was bulging suspiciously. 'The waiting is the worst part.' She felt more than a little apprehensive.

She was also in severe pain. Susanna had packed all of her medication in the wagon. Hopefully her exercises would help stretch out the muscles. She closed her eyes and began the slow stretching movements designed for her based on dance movements. She put the palm of her hand against the wall of the room for stability as she worked steadily through the routine. Mari felt a hand under her elbow and she opened her eyes.

'Use my shoulder. I'm more steady then the train.' Scott placed her hand on his shoulder just as the train jolted on the track. Without a word she kept working her left leg and then repeated everything with the right one.

When she had finished her exercises she squeezed his shoulder lightly. 'Thank you.' He took one look at her face and left the room. When he returned he had a very small amount of the whiskey in the bottom of a glass. 'Drink this.' He handed her the glass and she wrinkled her nose at the strong smell. She swallowed it in one gulp. 'How often do you need to stretch?' He asked taking the glass from her. He knew the alcohol would help for a small amount of time. 'As long as I have enough pain medication in my system I stretch every three days. Without it I do what I need to.' Mari's eyes communicated to him just how much pain she was dealing with in that moment.

Scott simply shook his head, 'You need to tell me when you're hurting. I dont know unless you say something aloud.' Mari nodded. She didnt trust her voice. No one had shown her this level of caring before. He kissed her forehead and helped her to the bed where she promptly curled up against the pillows. 'Sleep.' He told her then added, 'I'll wake you an hour before we have to get off the train.' The light disappeared as he headed back to stand watch in the living area.

Chapter Twelve - The Apartment

The only smell Scott could identify as they stepped off the train that morning was a strong scent of disinfectant. It was still very early and few people could be seen on the platform. Mari stayed exactly half a pace behind him at his elbow. She surreptitiously guided him through the station with subtle taps on his arm from underneath the sleeve of her cloak.

As she had suspected, John had some of his males posted at key points throughout the station. They were easily recognisable by the headsets John used for communications and a uniform of black trench coats. Mari kept her eyes down cast and followed Scott down the street past the waiting taxi cabs before touching his arm and guiding them into an alley out of sight. She watched as he made sure they hadn t been followed.

When he returned to lean against the brick wall of the building opposite her she assumed they were in the clear. Mari shrugged off the cloak she was wearing to reveal her tunic and pants ensemble. She had a greater range of movement while wearing it. Mari covered her elaborately styled braid with a matching head wrap.

She slipped her stick into the loops of the military type carry all that Rebekah had given to her. As she tucked a small knife into her boot and another into the belt at her waist she noticed Scott watching her with undisguised interest.

'You look like you re arming yourself for war.' He commented as she pinned the head wrap in place with what looked like sharpened hair pins. She didn t reply as she slung the bag back onto her back. Her movements had had a well-practised quality to them. He wondered briefly if she had had need of her fighting skills in this part of the city before.

As she stepped back into her position at his elbow she spoke in a low voice, 'Do not use my name if we are stopped for any reason.' Mari looked up at him and then back at the station expecting trouble at any moment. Scott touched her chest briefly. She looked up at him her silver eyes glowing slightly.

'Kimana. Your name is Kimana. ' *Beautiful butterfly* she translated to herself in her head. She returned his gesture by resting her hand gently on his chest briefly and speaking his name, 'Alek.' If she had to call him something else she wanted it to be a name with a powerful meaning. Alek was the defender of all. A powerful historical figure who had worked as hard as Anna to give the human race a chance to survive.

Scott looked around the corner both ways before leading her back into the early morning half-light. The streets were still strangely deserted. No one seemed to be about at all even though he could make out vague shadows moving behind the windows of both the grocery and bakery stores they passed. He assumed that the day in the city started much later than it did on the farm. Scott felt her nudge him slightly again. Although she had given him rough directions to her apartment every time she seemed to get spooked she would indicate that they should turn.

When they stood in front of a white stone building in a nicer part of the city she said in a low voice, 'This one.' She had possibly led him through every back alley and doubled back on herself half a dozen times. Scott had told her not to take chances and she never had when it came to the necessity of keeping her apartment a secret.

The full light of the sun was shining into the dome. The city was stirring around them. Mari put her hand on the biometric scanner and stood still for the full body scan. The door clicked open and Mari led Scott through the entry way to the living quarters. Nothing was out of place. It looked undisturbed.

She let out an inaudible sigh of relief. The apartment was decorated in the same soothing way as her rooms in both Mercy House and the farm. Scott stood in the middle of the large space scanning the room for entry points and visible weaknesses. She knew he would probably go over it more thoroughly after he had gotten comfortable with his surroundings.

Mari put the coffee machine on and took off her head wrap. She hoped coffee would put him at ease since she had decorated her home with the best of everything her money could buy. 'This is your bolt hole?' he asked turning to face her. Everything was open plan except for the bedrooms and cleaning area.

'I prefer the term safe house.' Mari could see he was still uncomfortable. She couldnt provide him with the wide open spaces he was used to. Her apartment had been designed to fit the maximum amount of luxuries in a limited space. He looked like a wild animal trapped inside a high fashion store. She took pity on him. 'Here.' She limped over to an overstuffed chair and put his coffee down on the side table beside it. She moved back to the small kitchen and put another cup in the machine for herself.

Scott looked around the large room. She'd decorated in silver, greys and different shades of greens. The softly filtered light reflected off the blue accents in the room. Somehow Mari seemed to fit right in. He watched as she limped over to the chair by the large arched windows. 'One way windows,' She explained, 'I can see out but no one can see in. Triple strengthened for defense. No bullet can penetrate and shatterproof.'

He was beginning to glimpse the confident woman she could be. She had been unsure in the territories as she had been learning their ways. He slowly drank his coffee and began to relax. Mari looked out at the new day. She had only been away a short time. They wouldn't be able to do anything until after dark. It would be easier to slip through the city without recognition then. 'We can't get closer until after dark.' She informed him.

'Mercy House?' He asked. 'Mercy House.' She confirmed, 'Late tonight after the performance and before the main doors are locked we can slip in through the kitchens.' She leaned forward in her chair, 'I think that's how Nick and Susanna got in.' They watched the people walk by the building for a while before Scott placed the empty mug back on the side table beside his seat and leaned forward, 'Tell me about Elanna.'

'I only met her that once really. What do you want to know?' Her fingers went to the pins in her hair. He watched as she uncoiled her braid and loosened her hair until it was hanging free. She was obviously uncomfortable with the subject he had chosen. Scott tried to soothe her as he said calmly 'Just your memories. Impressions. Anything you think that he might use against you.' He watched as her back straightened and she let herself re-member the woman who she had called mother.

'I looked just like her. A mirror image in fact. She inspected every inch of me to make sure.' Mari shuddered. 'I think her hair was darker but she seemed happy to see mine had turned such a pale shade. I felt like she was manipulating the situation to her own means and I think that was how she lived her life. John was besotted with her. Somehow she had wrapped him around her little finger. He treated her like she was the most precious thing in the world to him...almost as if they had mated and yet she wore no marks. Elanna seemed happy to be getting out of the contract and she moved stiffly almost as if...maybe...as if he had hurt her badly.' Her forehead creased and she shook her head.

'What?' Scott noticed how her body language had stiffened.

'Her clothes didn't fit right.' Mari whispered, 'It was almost as if she'd just given birth or lost a lot of weight.' She struggled to remember more and as she did nothing made sense. She stood up and with the aid of her stick made her way back to the kitchen still thinking. Mari put her coffee cup back in the machine and stood with her back to the living area. Was there a child she didn t know about and if so what had happened to the baby?

Scott wrapped his arms around her from behind. He had moved silently. 'Thank you.' He said in her ear. He felt the tension ebb out of her body as she slowly relaxed back against him. 'All I have are those memories and impressions. Nothing else makes sense.' She said softly. He rested his chin on top of her head lightly before answering, 'I think part of his motivation is your mother may have been mated to him like you observed. But I think she was strongly motivated by money and not love. She could have given him a child and then substituted you into the contract to move on from him. I think John is furious you survived the fall and now that he knows you're alive he wants to silence you.' He felt the involuntary shiver that rocked her body. He held her until she had regained her composure.

He loosened his hold so she could turn around if to face him. When she finally did Mari laid her head against his chest to listen to his heart beat. She felt his fingers in her hair and Scott asked, 'Do women braid their hair so intricately so their curls and waves don't escape?' She laughed at the silly question designed to lighten her mood, 'No. It's so we look pleasing to our contracted males. When one is not allowed to cut her hair it is also a way of keeping it neat.'

'Does Susanna know of your custom?' Scott asked realizing how big a concession she had made for his mother. Mari wished she could make excuses for the female but she nodded her head. 'It was necessary. Oceania City has different customs than Spark City. They have exceptions to the rule. Such as to bring down a fever or when your contracted male no longer finds your hair pleasing or it has become unmanageable because of the length. She said Liana would most probably have worn her hair even shorter.'

Too much of women s lives were dictated by the rules of Anna and the whims of males here. She had heard Scott's thoughts on the subject but he had only seen the outer edges of the con-strictions. Anna's laws, designed to bring females security and safety had had the opposite effect. Every year the high council seemed to add to them making the lives of all females within the cities much worse. It felt wrong to be dressing and acting like a submissive female when she knew that he valued her for more than her ability to look pretty.

'Where do all the female children get sent to from the con-tracts?' Scott asked changing the subject slightly as she took her cup from the machine in front of her. She put it down on the bench and took his hand. She led him back to the windows and pointed at the central building with a large golden dome. 'They are there. One wing holds the administrative offices of the high council and the meeting room. The rest of that building is dedicated to the education and training of all the female chil-dren born of contracts in the training area for Spark City. They are housed in the next building over in apartments according to age with house mothers. I have heard that the conditions are not always quite ideal.'

She turned from the windows then leaving Scott to look out at the view while she dealt with their luggage. She moved the wall to reach the master suite behind them and began to pop open the storage panels in the wall. Scott pressed more panels and they opened quietly to reveal her extra sticks and knives. 'Do you train here?' She heard Scott ask as he discovered her small arsenal of weapons further up the room in the living area.

She moved the wall back silently and joined him as he inspect-ed one of the pairs of shoes she stored there. They seemed too thin and light soled to be of much use to him. 'Those were for dancing. I keep them to remind me that anything is possible.' She pressed on the panel next to the arsenal to reveal a stack of paper and a jar of pencils in all colours.

He looked down at her as she admitted, 'I design clothing in my spare time.' He took the stack of papers she offered him and began to flip through them slowly. He didn't know art or design but he knew weapons and mating marks. He held that one up. 'I know it's not my place to be designing those. Sometimes I just have to draw to clear my head.' She offered hesitantly as she peeked over his arm to see some of her best work in his hands as he said, 'You need to draw. No shame in that.'

He was looking at her rendition of the children getting ready for an evening performance. She had concentrated on the details making sure that he could almost hear the swell of the crowds, the rustle of the costumes and feel the children steady their breathing as they prepared to take the stage. One of the children looked remarkably like a smaller version of herself. As he looked at her she touched the paper, 'I like to remember moments in my life that bring me happiness.'

She pressed the panel that held the books she had had bound together. 'These are all the drawings that didn't end up in the fashion rooms.' Scott replaced the stack of pages and then picked up one of the books. He flipped through the pages depicting the early days of Mercy House and how she had personally looked after the children until she could no longer cope without house mothers of her own.

The next book showed the sketches and designs of the remodeling work she had had done to turn Montmercy house into the comfortable private facility it was now. There were portraits of each child as they arrived in the dormitories and self-portraits of her over the years. The only noticeable change about her over the years was the expression in her eyes. The emotions had ranged from raw pain right through to intense joy.

'I drew that last one the night I signed the pre contract with Susanna.' Mari touched the last page. Her expression told him how private those drawings were and he felt privileged to have been allowed to share her memories. 'They're beautiful. You see the world in ways others don't. Don't stop drawing.'

He replaced her last book as his stomach growled.   Surprised
by the noise she smiled, 'I don't have anything here unless
you like those packaged dehydrated meals.' He shook his
head, What's option number two?' 'We go out. There's a fairly
decent food place about three blocks closer to Mercy House.'
She started to slide the wall back to reveal the sleeping area, 'I
need a few minutes to get ready.' He nodded and waited till she
had closed the wall after her.

Mari opened the wall closet panel and chose one of the dresses
least like her usual style. It draped over one shoulder and twisted diagonally across her back. It was an electric blue creation
the fashion rooms had come up with as a present for her last
birthday. She rummaged around in the box on her bed head for
the appropriate accessories.

Scott closed most of the panels and then tested the sharpness
of the knife she had left lying out on the side table. He had
no doubt she was repeating her earlier performance and that
underneath whatever skirt she wore she had strapped at least
three weapons. He took a few moments to make himself look
presentable in the mirror hanging on the wall close to the kitch-
en before Mari returned.

Her hair was elaborately coiled again and she had used jewel
tipped hair pins that matched her dress. She had a lighter colour head covering draped around her neck like a scarf and had
slunga matching bag across her body. In her hands was another stick and he was fairly sure that there was a trick to that one
too.

'Ready?' She asked expertly wrapping her hair up so he couldn't
identify the colour. He was speechless for a moment. She
looked stunning. She slowly limped over to him and put her
hand on his chest. 'Snap out of it. You will see women wearing
much less then this everywhere we go.' 'Not what I was thinking. He managed to get out, You look beautiful.'

Her expression softened, 'Thank you. For your personal information though you will see females wearing much less then this
and they are contracted. Any level one or two will solicit you.
They wear gauzy head wraps and face paint. They have heavily
embroidered outfits that flash their stomachs. Those in training
do not show an inch of skin other than their faces.'

He swallowed before asking, 'What do those who are mated
wear?' Mari took a step back and spoke as if reciting something
unpleasant, 'They wear what their mates tell them to. If he pre
fers her to dress like a female for pleasure she will do so but her
hair will be uncovered and her face clean of paint. If he wants
her to keep her mate marks covered for his eyes only she will
do so. If he wants her mate marks to show at all times she will
dress in an outfit similar to this one but her hair will be uncovered.'

 'Got it.' He repeated back to her, 'Contracted or have been
contracted the head covering is tied like yours. In training and
nothing shows but the face. Mated means no head wrap but
dresses to please her male. Yes?' 'Yes.' She was glad that he
had gotten the differences so fast and wouldn't make an irrevo-
cable mistake his first time out with her. She put the knife away
that he had been testing and looked around the room.

The only things out of place was the two coffee mugs on the
counter. They would use those again when they returned she
rationalized. He took her hand and as they left she murmured
into his ear, 'Take a left then two rights and another left. One
tap means left. Two means right and one on the shoulder
means hide.'

Chapter Thirteen - Mercy House

They were halfway to the restaurant when she tapped his shoulder once for *hide*. Scott dragged her into the nearest alley behind a grocery store, placed an arm either side of her head against the wall and kissed her thoroughly. After a few minutes, they could hear the footsteps pass and he raised his head. In a low voice he asked, 'How do you know his men Kimmi?' He had called her *my little butterfly*.

'They guarded me when John was not around. Sometimes they stood on the thresh hold of the room he had caged me in and taunted me for the shade of my hair, or whatever position he left me tied up in for his pleasure. I have nightmares of it sometimes.' Mari's voice with tinged with the shame she felt whenever she remembered just how vulnerable she had really been.

He spoke directly into her ear, 'You have nothing to be ashamed of.' Scott had witnessed a particularly bad nightmare firsthand one night on the train. He had spent the entire night just listening to the words that poured out of her as she begged and pleaded to be set free. Shaking his head to dispel the memory he gave her a gentle hug before she peeked around his solid body to make sure it was safe to come out.

He continued scanning the alley and the street beside them

making sure no one was shadowing them. 'We will miss the lunch serving.' He said as a way to let her know they were on the move again. A noise at the end of the alley drew both their attention. A sad little figure had curled in on itself at their intrusion. Mari held up one finger to Scott and limped slowly toward the child.

She used her stick to crouch down and touch the child's head. 'Hello. I'm lost. Can you help me?' She looked up at Scott who had followed her to the end of the alley and then focused back on the child who was trying to hide in an old produce crate. 'So 'm I,' she barely heard the child whisper. 'How long have you been out here little one?' She asked in a calm voice resisting the urge to run her hands through the child's dirty hair. It was hanging in strings down to the thin shoulders. Scott though maybe a few days by the state of the clothing.

'Have you heard of Mercy House?' She asked trying again. As with many of the younger children she had found this one seemed to still be learning her words. She was sure that it was a miniature female child they had found. 'Yes.' the child looked up at them and Mari found the features entirely feminine. She held out her hand, 'We're going there right now. I know that there is a lot of room for children who have no place to go. I promise that if you don't like how things are you don't have to stay.'

The little girl unfolded from the produce crate she had wedged herself into and put her little hand into Mari's without a backward glance. 'Alec we are escorting,' Mari stopped and asked the little girl, 'do you have a name sweetheart?' They waited as the little face struggled to remember and finally came with, 'The lady called me Keilana when she yelled.' Mari placed her hand on the little one's head briefly as she looked up at Scott her face troubled. 'Bring her with you.' He knew she wouldn't be able to leave her behind. Keeping a soothing tone in her voice whenever she addressed Keilana, she led both the child and Scott to the big stone and glass building she had called home for so many years.

Scott could see that John definitely had left his men guarding Mercy House. Once they entered the foyer she led them to the desk and waited. 'Lady Mercy wishes to spend time with my chosen and asked to have you tell her that the afternoon light has shades of purple in it.' Scott addressed the young male clerk who turned to serve them. The clerk noticed Keilana and mentioned, 'Maybe the young miss could spend some time up in the daycare while she waits you to conclude your business with Madame.'

Scott tapped Mari's arm overtly giving her leave to speak, 'That would be most welcome thank you.' She kept her eyes down-cast as she spoke. She knew he hated the deference but in her world it was necessary. They waited as the desk clerk dialed both the daycare and her personal office. He repeated the message and received her automatic clearance. 'If you will step this way to Lady Mercy's personal elevator. There will be someone to meet you at both floors three and five.' He pressed the buttons inside for them then stepped out again before the doors shut. As they came to floor three Mari quietly ushered them into the business level and waited by the entry doors.

The quietness of the room enveloped her and the calm she had been faking returned. 'I can take the child up to the dormitory level for you.' one of her newest business level employees stood in front of them with a smile. Keilana tightened her grip on Mari's hand and she used her stick to crouch down to the same height as the little girl, 'This is a good place. No one is going to hurt you or frighten you here. The only thing you will need to do straight away is get cleaned up and dressed into a new set of clothes.' She gave Keilana a gentle smile, 'Then you can play with the toys.'

At the word *toys* she dropped Mari's hand and held it out to the young woman beside them who promptly whisked Keilana back into the elevator. As the doors closed behind them Scott helped her to stand upright again.

'You always had a way with everyone around you Lady Mercy.

Welcome home.' They turned and found a young woman with a dark complexion and stunning electric blue eyes waiting for them. She led them to into another elevator. 'I see you found another stray on your way home.' The younger woman shuffled her armful of files as Mari loosened her head wrap. 'It's how I found you and everyone else working here Jo.' Mari looked at Scott, 'Scott Jackson meet Joanna Mercy my personal assistant.'

Jo's blue eyes swept over him from head to toe in a long look and she sighed dramatically, 'Tell me this is the one you're contracting with. Do they breed them all that gorgeous out in the territories?' Scott raised an eyebrow at Mari but kept silent. 'Manners Jo? I know Lilli tried to instill correct behavior into you.' Her words were slightly remonstrative with a smile on her face. She had missed her disrespectful friend. Jo laughed lightly with a toss of her head, 'I know and they didn't quite take. This is the penthouse level.' She added the last bit as a courtesy for Mari s guest.

The doors opened and Scott followed the women out into the foyer. 'I had security change one wall of the main room for me while you were gone.' The younger woman's face was serious now all traces of levity disappearing in a heartbeat. As they rounded the corner Mari came face to face with a wall of screens showing surveillance feeds from every area of the building. Mari approved immediately pointing to the four screens where she could spot the intruders instantly, 'Have they penetrated past level three or do they just watch the public access areas?'

'The only way up to three is the elevators and security has crawled all over them with a fine tooth comb.' Jo looked at Mari, 'You know I found him in your private office I put that in my report but he hasn't been seen near Mercy House since.' Mari took off her head scarf and with a flick of her forefinger gave Jo permission to remove hers also. Jo looked up from the screens again and registered Mari's appearance for the first time. 'Your hair?' the shock was evident in her voice as she circled around her to get the full effect. 'It's been cut.' She added with horror.

'I ran into John Smythe in Bordertown two days ago. He found me Jo. When he saw me again he threatened my life and the life of the person I was with. When we withdrew to the hotel he was whispering in the ears of anyone who would listen to him which made it impossible for us to leave. The only way out of town was to change my appearance and to pretend to be another female.' The two friends moved from the screens to the formal seating area leaving Scott to watch the feeds so that they could continue their conversation with a semblance of privacy.

'You did what you had to do to survive.' Jo cocked her head to the side and her mass of long unruly violet hair shifted like a waterfall, 'I must be rubbing off on you then.' Mari noticed a small black dot on the hand that had been holding Keilanas tiny one. She made a keep talking motion to Jo as she tapped Scott on his shoulder. Jo brought her up to date on the day to day running of Mercy House while Scott examined it. Before peeling it off her hand and squashing it under the heel of his boot. 'Your bracelet should have jammed the signal but I think we should be leaving soon.' He examined the screens again watching for any changes to the patterns of the men outside.

'He used the child to get to me. She was a trap.' At her expression Jo reached for her and gave her a fierce hug. 'Fight first. Cry later boss.' Scott privately agreed with her and watched as they rolled back and area rug to reveal a floor safe. 'What do you need?' Jo asked as she pressed her thumb print to the lock. Mari opened the safe and her bag at the same time. 'Its best you don't know. Just in case our friends down there storm the tower after I'm gone.' She took out a couple of pre wrapped packages and then shut the safe again.

Mari gave Scott her stick to hold and pulled an identical one from a rack on the wall. She took a swift look around the room as she pickedup a backpack from the floor of a closet and also handed it to Scott who promptly put it on. 'We're out of time.'

He nodded at the crowd building on the stairs of her building. 'Can you handle this?' Mari asked Jo as they hurried through the penthouse to the staircase to the private rooftop gardens.

The young woman nodded, 'Of course I can. Just need your new phrase for next time you want to catch up.' Scott answered as Mari started to climb, 'The black ring has tightened.' Jo looked up at Mari who was struggling up the stairs, 'Please tell me he's kidding.' Mari shook her head as she swiftly covered her hair up again with her head wrap, 'I don't think he knows how. Keep them all safe including the new little one.'

With those words she was out the door. Scott gave Jo a parting nod and disappeared. The door shut quietly after them.

Chapter Fourteen - Together

Mari looked over the edge of the building at the front entry to Mercy House. She could see the men gathering on the steps below. She drew back as one of them looked up. She moved to the opposite side of the building and scouted the next building over. As she turned around to face Scott she instructed quickly, 'Press the button but give yourself space.' She demonstrated for him and he watched fascinated as her stick extended at either side. It transformed into the double handle of a zip line bar.

It came complete with shackle to clip onto her chosen cable. She zipped up the interior of her bag and clipped onto a line that seemed to have no purpose other than run from her roof to the one she had just scouted. 'See you on the other side.' Mari took off at a limping run and hung on for grim life as she soared over the heads of the men who had been sent to find her who were just starting to filter around the back of the building to enclose it in a human barricade.

Scott watched her sail onto the roof and tuck into a roll before he followed her. She had removed her stick and was silently collapsing it back down when he bounced up out of his tuck roll. He copied her process and stuck them both through one of the loops on her pack. 'Ready?' he asked as she stood. She nodded and he followed her through the new building to the ground level. Keeping to the shadows she said, 'Four blocks south and then two lefts.'

She shivered at something and he read fear in her eyes. He turned quickly blocking her from view of everyone on the street. John was talking with his men in plain sight. He had dressed to blend in with the citizens of Spark City and was wearing a headset.

Scott edged her back into the building and they exited through the back of the building. He kept them moving swiftly through the back streets until they reached her apartment again. Just as they arrived at her building the noisy hum of a surveillance drone broke Mari's concentration. 'Get under cover quick.' Scott didn't look back as he pushed her into the small lift. Just as the doors closed they could hear the drone hovering right in front of the building.

He was not sure what the tech capabilities were but Mari was hurrying with her biotech locks. 'Scanning for thermal.' she said shortly as she opened the door. 'Quick the outer walls are lead lined.' He pulled the door shut after him and kept watch near a window until the drone disappeared.

The drones were used by the high council's enforcers and Mari knew that sometimes John s team hacked into their surveillance feeds. Hopefully all they had filmed was the back of her head as they entered the apartment. She stood with both hands on the kitchen bench holding herself upright with some effort. For a split second she thought that John had actually seen her in the street until Scott had blocked her from his view. She took a deep breath as Scott put the backpack in front of her and removed the sticks from the loop on the bag. She took one and leaned it up against the bench beside herself.

When she looked up at him she noticed that he was focused on the spare stick in his hand. It was light and functional for a walking cane but somehow she had managed to design it to have a double function. Scott had no idea how she had designed it but he knew that if she wanted to go into making weaponry for their community he would be proud to build her a workshop in one of the farm sheds.

Mari sank into the closest overstuffed chair in the living area. She lifted the shoulder bag she had been carrying over her head and removed the two packages from inside of it. Scott dragged a leg rest closer to her so she could be more comfortable and watched as she took a folding knife from her boot. She slit the edges of both packages carefully and began to lay out the contents on her lap. One held a lot of documents and the second held a significant amount of money, pain killers and expensive looking flat jewelry boxes.

Scott walked into the kitchen and when he returned he handed her a mug of water so she could take the tablets. He watched as she swallowed them and then focused again on the belongings on her lap. 'These are the jewels of my foremothers.' She touched one of the cases with distaste. 'They're not something I would choose to wear for any occasion but as with most old things I assume at one point they were the height of fashion.' Mari sighed as she showed him the heavily set blood rubies in one set.

She closed the lid of the case and explained, 'Upon a transition from contract to mating it is the tradition of my line to have a set of jewelry made to wear with their mating dress. I was not sure whether I would ever have the opportunity to continue the tradition.' She put them on the coffee table. 'The money?' Scott asked.

'Mostly blood money from my payout at the end of my last contract. The high council made sure I received extra for my pain and suffering.' She handed him a stack, 'For Rebekah.' He put it on the table in front of him. 'I didnt mean to offend.' She said quietly understanding quickly how she had made him feel, 'I just thought we could use it to help take care of her in some way.'

Mari knew that she needed to give him time. She sat quietly allowing the medication to take effect. She had not really paused to think about the things that had happened in the space of the last 72 hours. 'No sadness.' Scott's voice startled her out of her revelry. She looked at him as he leaned forward in the chair opposite her.

'You have nothing to feel bad about. This is your world and I reacted badly.' He reached across the table and took her hand. Mari looked down at their joined hands and then back up at him. 'This money did not bring me solace or peace.' She stated softly and shook her head. Her heart felt too full of all the emotions that would not be helpful in this moment. She watched as he picked up the money with his other hand and put it in one of his inner jacket pockets. 'We will use it to take care of Rebekah as you suggested little one.'

'Little one?' She repeated a smile creeping over her face. 'It felt natural.' Scott shrugged relieved that he had managed to bring back her smile. He watched as she turned to the stack of paperwork flipping through the pages until she found what she was looking for. 'What are they?' Scott indicated the pages she had discarded into another neat pile. Mari replied, 'The deed to Mercy House, the deed for my apartment, my family lineage including all contracts and sons going back five generations, the high council's decision regarding my last contract and our contract.'

She placed her hands in her lap and looked at him. 'I have chosen you Scott Jackson. Will you formalize the contract between us so that we may take it before the high council for approval?' Scott silently thanked Susanna for giving him a crash course in the intricacies of the contract and all the formal responses required. 'Marianna de Montmercy it would be an honor to treasure you within this contract's bounds and hope for a mated outcome.' he answered just as formally.

'Do you wish to read the amendment section before you sign? I had Joanna add one to the contract after our last talk just in case.' She wished she knew if she was conducting these formalities correctly. Her memories of her signing last time were clouded with holes. Mari removed her contacts just as he removed his glasses. She handed over the document in full and he flipped to the short page of amendments which he read silently to himself.

Scott was more than satisfied with the amendments she had added to the original contract. Mari had rephrased the terminology and taken all his requests to heart. 'Should Susanna be here to witness this?' He asked knowing that such things were usually handled by mothers and foremothers. She picked up the pen and answered 'No but the high council will need to formally acknowledge that this contract between us not only exists but has their approval.' Mari began to lower the pen when he stopped her again, 'Are you satisfied with the contract as a whole including the amendments?'

'You have offered me more than what I am legally allowed to put on paper. We need to convince the high council that this is a contract that they can accept within the laws of Anna. ' Her silver eyes met his green ones before they dropped back to the table as she signed her parts of the contract and dated it. He added his signatures at the appropriate places and placed the pen back on the coffee table between them. Mari stored the contract back in her bag along with most of the money she had removed earlier. She limped over to store it in one of the wall panel cupboards closest to the door. He caught her hand and pulled her to him gently as she walked close by.

'Let down your hair for me.' He heard himself say. She sat in his lap and slowly removed her head covering. She slid the scarf from around her neck and draped it around his pulling him close with the two ends for a lingering kiss. As he leaned back in the chair she removed the pins and one by one the intricately braided coils fell. He watched as she lifted her hands and ran her fingers through her hair until it hung free.

'You are beautiful.' He slid his hand through her hair. It felt like silk flowing through his fingers. Scott ran his other hand down her neck and across the top of one of her shoulders. He was exploring the female he finally had the right to call his. He could feel her slowly relax as he ran a hand over her back lightly rubbing it in soothing circular motions.

She felt her nerves disappearing as she leaned closer to his body finally resting her head against his shoulder. His fingers brushed under the edges of the material of her dress when he finally asked, 'Where are your bruises?'

He turned her arm over inspecting the unblemished skin. 'Right there still. I used skin cover to cover them up.' At his raised eyebrow she added, 'The healers gave me a spray to conceal my scars until I got used to them. I had some hidden here for an emergency.' Scott ran his fingers over the entire area lightly and watched as she still couldn't hold back a flinch of pain. 'Let's get this taken care of.' He wanted to keep exploring her but her wellbeing would always come first.

It was with some reluctance that he watched her slide off his lap. He watched as she made her way over to another moveable wall. He pushed it back for her to reveal a neat workshop and office combination. She retrieved a bandage and cleaning wipes from another panel in the wall by her desk.

He looked at project on her desk still in pieces. 'I could never quite figure out how to make this one work without causing harm to myself.' She ran a fingertip over the stick she had in a cradle. Scott looked at the blue print she had pinned over the table showing the intent and broken down design. 'You are trying to fit the concept of a pipe bomb in a stick.' He was stating the obvious taking the wipes from her hands. From the little he had known of the dome dwellers he knew they were a peaceful people. He looked at Mari and smiled at least on the surface anyway.

She had no longer seemed suited to the tame life inside the

dome city. 'I thought that if I needed a large diversion one of these might come in handy.' She mused obviously lost in her work within moments. Scott looked it over, 'I'll take a look at it and see if I can give you any suggestions.' His time in the turbine sheds working with the farm machinery would come in handy. He was in love with her fascination with weaponry and concealment. He wondered how she had found the time to do everything she had accomplished between Mercy House and the amount of preparation she had put into her survival.

'How did you manage it to balance such a busy life?' He asked putting the supplies down on the table and maneuvering her into the light so he could see what he was doing. 'I didn't sleep much. In the early years the nightmares wouldn't let me and after a while it became habit.' He wiped off the area to reveal the marks now ranging in shades of blue, black and purple. 'I think the best way for this to heal is for you not to be using this arm at all.' He looked up from his work.

'We need to blend in and wearing any kind of a sling will make me stand out even more. I can't wear hooded cloaks in the middle of the day. 'Mari replied. She was feeling hunted and she didn't like the feeling one bit. She focused on the stick in the cradle again. 'I need to be able to fight.' She shifted her eyes back to Scott's face, 'John is devious and he will use whatever means it takes to subdue me. ' 'So let's use this against him. ' Scott thought fast, 'He has already hurt you and the Elders don't like that sort of thing. When can we submit our copy of the contract to the high council?'

They hadn't been in the city for an entire day and he already knew he needed to get Mari home. Scott needed the real word around him. Fresh air. He had been raised to identify everything by sound and smell. There was always something hidden in the shadows. He never trusted things at first glance. He watched as she silently tried to remember the protocol surrounding lodging a contract. 'We have to leave in the next few days if we want to beat the weather.' Scott refastened the bandage with a small clip.

'We can lodge the paperwork straight away but we will have to wait to see if high council calls us to answer any further questions while they in session.' Mari spoke finally. Her expression said a lot more. They were going to have to be ready for anything if that happened. She knew John wouldn't hesitate to manipulate the situation to his best interests if it meant gaining control over her again.   '

'Tomorrow.' Scott thought. It could wait till tomorrow. She could barely stand even with the aid of her stick. He could see a few small cuts on her arms from the tuck roll she had been forced to do earlier. Tonight she would need to rest. They moved back through the living space and he replaced the wall so she could access the kitchen. Mari picked up her discarded head covering and Scott tied it into a sling that he slipped over her head so she could rest her arm. 'Unless that drone got a fix on our position tonight you are going to rest that arm.' He was firm as she turned to face him with a protest on her lips. At his fierce look she gave in with good grace.

After they had eaten Mari curled up in one of her comfy armchairs. Scott had proved to be just as creative with the dehydrated food packs as she was. He had retreated to the work room to take another look at the design she had in progress. He could see what she was trying to achieve within a few moments of looking over both the parts she had laid out neatly on the table and the blue print. 'Did you want to twist the handle or press the button?' He asked as she drew in the fading light. Mari looked up from the portrait of him she was working on. 'Twist. I don't accidentally want to depress the button and blow us up instead.'

The overhead lights automatically turned on as the evening set in. Mari looked up realizing just how much work went into something she had previously taken for granted. Her short stay in the territories had changed her view of what hard work really was. She bowed her head again and went back to her drawing. The silence stretched for a couple of hours until Scott finally stood up and stretched. On the work table in front of him lay a new weapon to be field tested when it was needed. All he had done was figure out how to arm the stick safely.

Mari had fallen asleep with one of her books on her lap. He quietly stood beside her contemplating what she had drawn. All across one page were different images of him. She had captured a group drawing of all of them from the confrontation with John. He was standing at her back, knife drawn with a deadly look on his face. He hadn't realized that she had had that much time to take in all the details. She had looked so focused on John. Underneath she had written the word *protected*.

There was the night he had finally opened up to her in the garden at home. She had once again left out no details and he read the caption *honest*. Then the last picture showed Rebekah's basement with her wrapped up in a blanket on his lap. The sadness on her face touched him all over again and he read the caption *wanted*.

She was a gift within herself he mused. She saw everything around her in perfect clarity and sought only to make things better. He looked at the image of the confrontation again and noticed that even when he thought she wasn't protected she had been holding weapons ready to use. He thought about her statement earlier about needing to be able to fight. She wanted to keep him safe as much as he did her. That touched his heart in places where nothing had for a very long time.

She moved in her sleep and her hand opened. He removed one of her precious pencils before it dropped to the floor and broke. She would not be able to get those easily out in the territories. He would have to make sure Jo sent them a new set each season. Mari opened her eyes as he scooped her up in his arms then shut them again. 'Feels like you're always doing this.' She said sleepily.

Scott wasn't sure if she was awake or asleep but he answered anyway, 'Doing what beautiful?' 'Taking care of me in my sleep.' She opened her eyes as he put her down gently on the bed. Her bi colored hair streamed across the pillows. 'That's because it's my turn.' he said quietly. Not to mention his right as her contracted male. He would take the day shift too once they got back to the territories but until then he conceded he would follow her lead.

Mari sleepily digested this news as she reached under the pillow next to her for her sleeping clothes. She sat up and made her way slowly to the cleaning room. She had never been able to forego her evening shower. It was a large part of her evening ritual before bed. Scott waited until she had seated herself and her hands were at the tie at the back of her dress. 'I'll wait out in the kitchen.' He didn't know how much longer he would be able to give her the privacy Susanna thought she would need to settle into a new contract. He shut the wall behind him and busied himself making hot drinks.

When she opened the wall again he had a mug of tea ready for her. She eyed him from over the rim of the mug. She put it down on the side table and said, 'This is a small apartment. I'm not sure how long one must be courting before you share your naked bodies. If we are to be here for a while this could become an issue.'

So she had noticed him giving her her space. Susanna and Nick had obviously read her wrong. She took his hand, 'I'm not ashamed of my body or the scars I bear.' So had he obviously. Scott finished his mouthful. He had thought about how to answer her when this subject came up. He knew that she had felt him pull back earlier that afternoon.   '

'You feel right in my arms with your head on my chest.' He admitted choosing his words carefully as this was a delicate subject, 'I'm not avoiding you.' She waited quietly knowing this went much deeper then cultural differences. He took both of her hands, 'Your last contract was a bad one. I'm no saint but I can give you time to get used to me. I want this to be the start of something good for both of us.'

Mari could understand that. She squeezed one of his hands as she looked up at him, 'Then let's keep it good. Will you sleep under the cover with me tonight?' At his look she added, 'Just hold me. I like being in your arms. Your heartbeat is comforting.' She felt safe there. It was at that moment she understood what the word *cherished* meant.   He cupped her face and asked softly, 'You're sure.' Mari nodded her head silently. Had he been a part of the contract negotiations he would have had the option to view her body. It was usual practice to go straight from a signing to a bedroom.

Courting had many different nuances that she had yet to learn. She picked up her mug and took another sip. Scott swallowed. He hadn't dared hope that she would invite him into her bed so soon. He had been surprised when she had asked him to join her on it in the train. 'Give me a few minutes to get cleaned up.'

It was close to midnight when Mari slipped from the bed and retrieved her com from a panel in the living area. She knew Jo would still be up likely finishing the last of the day's paperwork or drinking. One never knew where Jo was concerned but she was good with people and that was what mattered most.

They would need an escape plan if John showed up at the high council building. Mari shuddered to think what might happen if he managed to get within the inner chambers themselves to literally challenge the very words of the contract itself. She keyed a quick message,

'Need you to show at high council before first session. Possible?'

A reply came back almost immediately.

'Definitely. I can bring some brothers with me.'

'J back in play. Bring your boys but keep them leashed.'

It wouldn't do to create too big of a public scene. There were too many children moving between classes to consider as well as all the elders. Mari rubbed her temples with her finger tips before putting her com away. She tiptoed back to bed before she was missed.

Watching the city come to life had long been one of Mari's many habits. She had been quietly packing her apartment into travel bags when Scott made an appearance the next morning. Two large duffle bags sat against the wall nearest to the door already waiting. He poured himself some coffee and joined her as she opened the bag they had brought back from Mercy House. She shook out a lavender dress with a royal purple sash that matched her hair exactly. The dye had completely washed out that morning under the shower. He watched bemused as she pulled out matching dainty shoes and a multitude of accessories as well.

'When you are invited into a high council session it is considered a most formal occasion. Your best clothes and manners are required.' She explained as she laid out a formal outfit for him consisting of dark dress pants and a deep blue long sleeved dress shirt. Fancy shoes appeared from the recesses of the bag as well. 'I had Jo get these from the fashion rooms for us. It will take me a little extra time to get ready. Cereal bars are in the dry food cupboard.'

Scott watched as she limped into the bedroom. He would bet his best throwing knife that she had already contacted Jo and they were in cahoots about something to do with their upcoming morning. He heard her in her work room a while later rummaging in the storage cupboards there.

'Weaponry?' He asked as she reappeared. He knew she was too smart to go anywhere near John Smythe without a way to protect herself, 'Nothing obvious.' She replied with a small smile. She continued past him putting a pair of stud earrings into her ear lobes. 'Your lipstick is hallucinogenic?' Scott guessed earning him a raised eyebrow. She laughed a tinkling laugh before replying, 'Nothing that sophisticated.'

'My brooch is a throwing star. The tips of my hair pins hold a knock out serum and my stick extends to a staff. I've had to tone it down a bit since we are going to the high council after all.'Her grin was a completely evil one.

'Knock out hairpins.' Scott was seriously impressed. She had a completely devious mind when it came to her weaponry and he loved it. 'Knock out hairpins.' She confirmed showing him one as she started to work her hair into a more formal elaborate hairstyle that formed a crown of hair and left the back hanging free. As she reached for the head covering Jo had provided he stopped her. 'Leave it off.' Scott took the scarf from her and wrapped it over the bandage making it look like it was a natural part of her outfit. He stood back from her and pronounced, 'Prettier than a picture.' Thank you.' She blushed and handed him his outfit complete with all the required city gentleman's accessories, 'Nothing here is any different from what you normally wear. I had Jo steer away from the more cutting edge choices that she might have gone for.' She watched as he disappeared behind the wall.

Mari began transferring the papers required for that morning as well as some paper coin to the matching silk purple sling bag Johad found for her. She hadn't told Scott about the weapons she had hidden in her underwear. In fact, she hadn't been lying to Nick when she had said she wore Kevlar underwear.

It was a one-piece garment that resembled swimwear with inbuilt sheaths for two thin extremely sharp stiletto knives that she could easily access from her bodice if needed. Her earrings were tiny little smoke bombs. The 'pearl' was easily detached and all she had to do was throw it at something hard enough to break it.

She still needed a couple of tricks up her sleeve just in case they were separated for any reason. Scott watched as she filled the empty backpack with a stack of clothes she had taken from the bedroom while he was sleeping. He cleared his throat and she looked up. She stopped what she was doing and said with a dry mouth, 'Completely gorgeous.'   Standing in front of her was a man who was confident enough to navigate the wilds of the city as well as survive everything the territories could throw at them. He gave her a knowing smile before holding out his hand to her with one eyebrow raised, 'Ready?'

Mari

He gave me a warm smile but as we faced the door I could feel him reverting back to the way he had been the day we had first met. He squeezed my hand gently as if to remind me that he was only donning the hard persona to protect me from John Smythe and whatever tricks the high council may try.

I squeezed his hand back hoping to convey the message that I wasnt afraid and I knew that no matter what happened I wasnt alone. We walked. He walked. I limped a half step behind him using my walking stick trying to keep up with his long strides as best as I could.

When he realised that I was having trouble matching his long stride he stopped and waited. His eyes were ice cold as he scanned either side of the street as if expecting an ambush on the way to the heart of the city. I wished we had the time for me to show him my favourite place in Spark City.

I so wanted to show him the exquisite gardens where something beautiful could be discovered just around every corner. The very same gardens where Susanna had purposely made contact with me. They looked like nothing that could be found outside in the territories.

Maybe one day we would be able to relax in the sun and not always be on our guard with weapons close to hand.

Chapter Fifteen - The High Council

The High Council building had a facade of impressive stone. It looked as if it had once been white but time had worn it down into a respectable grey. Scott thought the building still looked formidable and solid enough to last another three hundred years. He placed Mari's hand in the crook of his arm as they began to climb the steps into the building.

They'd had to pause once in their journey between her apartment and the building. He had not noticed her struggling to keep in step with him to preserve the silly city rituals. She had turned her expressive silver eyes on him. Brief sadness had crossed her face for a moment and he had wondered what she had been thinking. He hoped that he had not been the cause of that pain.

He helped her up the last few steps and into the antechamber where Jo met them with three men shadowing her every step. He drew Mari under his arm as he evaluated what threat they posed. None of them bore a passing resemblance to any other. 'Ed, Cerin and Reece. They are my brothers of the heart.' Jo introduced them pointing covertly as she went. 'Mari and Scott. No one with anything resembling a compass tattoo gets close. She saved my life. She's family.' Jo had dressed in her street clothes of skin tight pants, calf high boots and a hooded shirt under a leather jacket for the occasion. As usual her wild hair was attracting too much attention and she flipped her hood up to hide it without too much thought.

Mari edged closer to Scott as she noticed the various looks they were attracting. The antechamber was full of males wishing to petition the high council. Jo's brothers instantly closed in around them so that their conversation remained private. 'Nothing will touch you today boss. I promise.' Jo hugged Mari. 'Go do your thing. We've got your back.' She added off handedly with a cheeky grin, 'You look great. He looks absolutely amazing.'

Jo gave Scott a measured look. It was one he almost couldn't decipher until she said for his ears alone. 'If he gets past my shadows don't let her fight him here. Better this is the day she's never had before and always wanted. Shit goes down later yeah.' Once things were finalized with the paperwork he would personally hunt this male down if he ever came after them again. Scott had an insightful feeling that this was not the first time that Jo and her boys had covered Mari while she was out in public.

Jo and her 'brothers' disappeared into the crowd milling around in the antechamber. Female children of different ages moved through the room in classes walking in crocodile formation. The only differences were the colors of their clothes and their heights. Mari tugged Scott's hand subtly and led him through to another section of the building.

A clerk looked up Mari's name on an electronic database as they submitted their signed copy of their contract. He tapped a message on his com and waited until it beeped a reply. They were escorted by an elder into a bright naturally lit room filled from floor to ceiling with books. The ceilings were painted and the floor laid in a busy tile pattern. 'This room hurts my eyes.' Scott spoke into her ear. Mari replied in a soft voice, 'It's meant to be impressive. Impressive and usually filled with Elders who can vote against our contract. I will speak for us in here.'

She moved to stand in front of the only desk in the room. A silver haired Elder in a red robe sat reading their contract in front of her through half-moon glasses. When she raised her head Mari curtseyed to her, 'Forgive me Elder Bryce but how can we be of further assistance to you.' She looked into the eyes of one of her favorite private tutors before quickly lowering them.

It would not do to shame her teacher in this the most sacred of public places. 'Marianna de Montmercy. I remember you.' the Elder's voice was strong despite the frailty of her body. 'Your file has been red flagged and your current contract is being scrutinized due to the debacle of your last one.'

Debacle. It was a nice way of saying that she had nearly died. Mari's eyes slowly lowered and Scott watched her slip back into the submissiveness that he had despised the most when he had met her. 'Am I being denied the intrinsic right to choose whom I wish to contract with?' She asked in a well moderated tone of voice nothing betraying her hidden emotions caused by the Elder's words. Elder Bryce looked up from her screen again and took note of the translucence of her skin, 'Not at all. I believe the Elder who put the flag on your file merely wished to have the council assure themselves of the male you were contracting with and add fine print that would assure us that your miraculous survival continued.'

Scott unclenched his jaw. His face had steadily grown more serious as he realized the under currents and eddies of the power struggle that was taking place. 'If it please the council I will answer on behalf of myself and my family.' Scott bowed to the woman half edging Mari behind him giving her time to breathe. The older female eyed him curiously. He had hidden Mari completely behind him within the space of a few seconds. She had no doubts that Mari would be treated with the respect and love due a mated female.

'Despite what you may think of me. She has done for the lost of the city what the constraints of my role within the council does not allow me to. Marianna is a credit to the laws of Anna.' Elder Bryce rose picking up their application off her desk, 'If you would be so kind as to wait here Mr. Jackson, I will present your case to the session room now. I'm sure you wish to get back home before you get cut off for the season.'

She disappeared through the shadowy doorway at the end of the room. He turned to assure himself that Mari was alright. 'She was playing with you.' Scott touched her shoulder to reassure her. She nodded, 'They will all play with us. We will not know whether our contract stands until the Madame speaker gives her final verdict.' She leaned heavily on her stick feeling weary of the hoops this city had made her jump through in order to live some semblance of a normal life after her accident. A credit to the laws of Anna indeed she thought to herself. At first she had taken in the children because she had been so lost herself and then she had trained them so that if they didn t want to follow the rules they didn t have to.

'You are someone precious to them. Contract or no. I will court you. Do you accept me?' Scott scanned her face for any clue of her response. He had asked her in the way of his people bringing her out of her deep thoughts. This was the only way he knew how to take her back with him and keep her a free woman. She had an inner strength stronger than he had ever seen in a female before but together they would be stronger. 'I accept.' Mari answered without hesitation and added, 'John will never stop coming after me now that he has found me again.' Scott took her hands, 'He is no longer only your concern. We are not alone in the territories. We have many friends and he has made many enemies. Don't be afraid of John Smythe.'

'Mr. Jackson, Marianna.' Elder Bryce reappeared in the doorway, 'They are ready for you now.'   There were two chairs on the stage of a half amphitheater and Mari whispered into his ear as they walked towards the stage, 'Keep your gaze straight ahead. Do not meet the Madame Speaker's gaze. Do not speak unless specifically addressed. Do not answer a question addressed to me. They don't like that. Bow deeply when I curtsey.' As they reached the entry to the council chambers Scott watched Mari give the most graceful curtsey he had ever seen. He bowed and Elder Bryce escorted them both to the seats. The elders were seated in three tiers all around the wall.

As Mari finished arranging her skirts the Madame Speaker of the high council brought the room to order, *'All discussion pertaining to the contract between Marianna de Montmercy and Scott Jackson is at an end. Questions concerning the petitioners may now begin.'* Mari dipped her head to her in respect. It had been the veiled Elder in dark navy who had dissolved her contract with John Smythe as soon as she had seen the damage that had been inflicted on her both body and soul during her first visit with her in the healing center.

'Mr. Jackson would you care to state the differences between contracting and courting.'

Scott replied only giving the high council what they needed to hear, 'I believe courting is to treat a female as someone you hold closest to your heart. To court is to show extreme respect. To contract is a legally binding document signed by other people on your behalf. To contract is for a female to be treated like a possession by all involved.'

'I don't believe Anna's laws turn females into possessions Mr. Jackson would you care to comment?'

Mari shot Scott a warning look. She remembered his words from the day they had met and she hoped he would be more circumspect with his thoughts on the subject here. They were treading on dangerous ground now. The council was trying to establish if the Jackson family were rebels against the laws of Anna.

He caught her look out of the corner of his eye and nodded very slightly to let her know he understood, 'I live in the territories my lady. You either have someone you're courting, a mate or you are property. Unless your family keeps you home and hidden from all who visit. Those are the only three options for females. Many are free born and do not attend your training schools. They all generally court with a view to mate. I do not wish to be disrespectful of Anna's laws but Anna herself never lived where I come from. The environment is harsh and men are bred rough. I believe this is the reason that there are two templates.'

She breathed a silent sigh of relief. He had come so close with the remarks about Anna but he did have a point and they would have to concede to it.

'Marianna you signed this contract of your own free will?'

'Yes my lady.' Mari waited for the next question as she was sure they had moved on from Scott now.

'You are very sure you wish to switch templates as stated in the amendments?'

'Yes my lady.' She looked at Scott when the noise of a commotion in the outer room overtook the deliberations of the elders amongst themselves. The doors to the room opened and males circled the stage. Mari chanced a look at Scott.

What had happened to Jo and her brothers? 'I wish to challenge the validity of this contract.' John's voice rang out loud and clear as he entered the Smythe towers balcony overlooking the tiers, 'My apologies for my late arrival but there was some opposition to my attending these proceedings.'

All heads turned as one to face the intruder. Hidden from the high council behind the wall of black Mari rested her hands serenely in her lap as she calmly waited for what he would say. Scott looked at her and knew she had evaluated the situation. He didn't like that they were surrounded and could do nothing other than listen to what was said.

'Please state your name for the high council.'

'John Smythe formerly of Spark City.' John looked smug as he made eye contact with the couple below him. He finally had Marianna just where he wanted her. She knew that no one ever escaped from him until he was ready to let them go.

'You were Marianna de Montmercys former contract.'

'Yes my lady.' John's face didn't change as he answered the council. Maybe he thought he was assured of success in challenging their contract. Mari wondered what his end game was. She knew that he had never truly wanted to contract with her and now he was there to prevent her future happiness. Did he really believe all females were placed upon this planet for his personal pleasure? She doubted the council would allow him to manipulate them into the outcome he desired without putting up a verbal battle.

'You were the contract that harmed her.'

The Elder who asked the question stood to face him with an accusing look upon her lovely face.

'No my lady it was a terrible accident.' John's brows drew together and Mari allowed herself a small smile. She had figured out the mind game they were playing with him. He had contravened the laws of Anna and they were establishing it for the records yet again.

'Explain if it was such a terrible accident why the imprint of the sole of your boot was found on Marianna's back?'

A second Elder stood up next to the first one and turned an accusing face at John.

Mari's smile widened. She had just noticed something that made her feel even more safer. Covertly she pointed at the men's compass tattoos and Scott raised his eyebrows.

The three men directly in front of them were not John's males. In fact, none of them truly were. They were something else. The compass tattoos were covering scars all placed in the exact same place on the males necks.

'Enough. What new evidence do you base your objection to this contract upon Mr. Smythe?'

Madame Speaker spoke with finality. Both females in red dipped their heads to her respectfully and sat down. Only the ticking of the clock could be heard above the silence as the whole room waited for his answer.

John opened and closed his hands on the balustrade before answering. 'Marianna de Montmercy was not free to enter into a new contract. If you check the fine print of her previous contract it states that if the contract between us should fail Marianna is mine to do with as I see fit for the rest of her natural life. She belongs to me in any capacity I choose.'

'Marianna do you wish to rebut this statement?'

Did she ever. Mari took in the whole high council as the wall of black stepped aside so they could view her as she responded. She controlled the hatred and anger thrumming through her body at his accusation. When she spoke her voice was calm and her tone was well moderated. She refused to let John bait her in front of the council.

'My Lady, Elders and those who stand here to witness. The fact that I lived under a contract with John Smythe is well established. As this high council is extremely aware Elanna de Montmercy tied me to this man with an illegal binding clause.

She manipulated me to meet her at Smythe Towers and then blackmailed me into remaining. I did not sign this contract and did not indicate my acceptance for Elanna to sign on my behalf.

Under the laws of Anna, no woman may be considered a slave. These laws exist to protect us. Because of the freedom clause Elanna used I was never safe. Because of this male I almost lost my life. This high council rendered the contract between myself and John Smythe complete with damages owing some ten years ago after the deaths of my daughter and birth mother.

Three days ago this male attacked me in Bordertown exposing my level for every male in the street to see. May I respectfully ask how under the laws that govern us all this male has the right to challenge a contract between myself and the Jackson family?'

'Under the laws of Anna the contract between Marianna de Montmercy and John Smythe was indeed completed with damages. Mr. Smythe have you any additional evidence to present that that renders your challenge valid?'

John glowered at Mari. He had never taken the time to get to know her as a person and he didn't like that she had outsmarted him. His men cut her off from view again as he answered, 'Our contract will never be completed. The laws of Anna cannot be forced upon the unwilling. Who are you to judge what a male may or may not do with his female? Heed my words the Way of the Eight will not stay hidden for much longer.'

The three males in front of Mari and Scott stepped out of formation. They surrounded them and one spoke directly into Mari's ear, 'The circle of black is tightening.' 'Jo?' asked Mari softly and he nodded. These were Jo's missing brothers. They kept Mari and Scott in their center and turned to fight their way out of the room if necessary.

Mari thought she glimpsed Jo as John turned to face something behind him. Scott witnessed Ed and Cerin holding a struggling John while Jo imparted something to him. It must have been something very close to her heart because he thought she was crying. Mari raised her hands to her mouth.

Her heart was pounding in her chest. Jo had a strange almost vindictive look on her face as she watched Reece deliver a boot to John's chest.

She heard someone scream as he fell heavily from the balcony to land on the floor in front of the tiers. Jo waved a gloved hand before smoke hid their retreat from sight. It was pandemonium as the room emptied of black uniformed bodies. In a daze she felt herself being picked up. Scott's voice said in her ear, 'I've got you.' She heard him say to someone, 'We will wait for the final decision. Let us know when you are ready to proceed.'

Healers pushed past them to check John's vitals. From what she could understand out of the discussion being held around her Johns body wasn't going to heal without extra help. Mari made no offer to have him checked into the Mercy House healing center. Scott turned her head away from the sight as they were escorted right past the group of people surrounding the prone body on the floor.

'You may wait in my personal retreat.' Madame Speaker herself personally led them out of the mostly cleared council chamber. Jo's brothers had formed a protection detail around them silently. As they entered the retreat the brothers took up post at the door. Scott put Mari down on her feet and waited till she had her balance. She remained silent until she was sure Madame Speaker had left the area.

Chapter Sixteen - Jo's Brothers

Scott waited until he was sure that she could stand on her own before taking a step toward the door. 'What do you know about Jo's brothers?' He asked her in a low tone. 'Not enough.' Mari replied. He watched as she opened the door and softly asked, 'How long did she ask you to keep guarding us?'

One male turned toward them, 'She didn t ask. Only Ed, Cerin and Reece answered her com. We've been watching out for you ever since you saved Jo from dying in the street.' Mari took a moment to process the new information. Jo had always said that they probably had three guardian angels watching their backs every time they went out to the rim tenements. Obviously she had underestimated her brothers and there had been more. She wondered what else Jo hadn't been kidding about. 'Thank you for your kindness.' Mari dipped her head to them.

'No, my lady don't.' Another of the men turned around to face her. This one had facial piercings and a glacial look in his eyes. She instinctively backed up a step into Scott. He stepped around her blocking a perceived threat. The male waited until Mari had composed herself enough to peek around Scott's shoulder. 'I did not mean to startle you.' He touched his face, 'I was once owned. The laws of Anna do not always mean much out in the rim. We protect you because we do not want to see Jo hurt. She says you re family and we protect our sisters.'

Sisters. Mari had never even seen one of the brothers before today. Jo had bragged that they were the best at their chosen specialties. Mari had always assumed that was street code for stuff she didn t want to know about. She was right. She felt ashamed by her actions and reached out a hand and touched him on his shoulder. 'You have been watching out for me and I was not aware of it. I know better than to let a few piercings startle me. You owe me no explanations. If anything I should be ashamed of my actions.'

The pierced male eyed Scott, 'That entitled SOB hurt her badly. Don't repeat his mistake. We're always going to have eyes on her.' Mari didn't like the threat. It was well intentioned but for all intents and purposes the brothers were still strangers to her. 'You know we're going back to the territories whether our contract stands or not right?' Mari asked her voice stronger, 'I agreed to the courting in the way of Scott's people.' They nodded tightly. The third brother turned to look at them as the other two turned back to watch the crowd forming in front of the council room.

'Take Jo with you.' He looked Scott in the eyes. Mari felt the menace emanating from him like a cold chill to her very bones. 'Explain.' Scott stood his ground. Mari drew her knife silently 'She does better around Lady Mercy. You've turned my hell cat into a lady. It won't be a good fit if she has to move back to the rim.' Scott couldn't help laughing. The male braced his feet for a fight.

'Mari. Show him.' He stepped aside so they could see her. Mari watched the male's eyes take in everything from the way she was standing to the knife she was holding at the ready. She raised an eyebrow at them as she slowly lowered her weapon. 'She might be a lady but she's a deadly adversary. I've seen her fight my father. If she had not been feeling in a merciful mood, he would have been singing soprano for the rest of his life.'

Mari sheathed the knife in her bodice raising an eyebrow as the male reddened slightly. 'The dress didn't come with weapon holsters. Take it up with Jo,' Mari gave him a steady look. 'She will always have a home at Mercy House. I plan on opening a healing center in Bordertown. When that happens she will be the first person I contact about a job. Until then she is Lady Mercy.' The brother nodded once showing her his instant respect. He had never seen her with weapons before and damn if she hadn't twirled the stiletto knife expertly before sheathing it.

'Why have none of you introduced yourselves to me before?' Mari asked aware that time was slipping away from them. She was supposed to playing the role of a helpless female and it wouldn't do for the high council to catch her showing who she really was. The male before them crossed his arms. 'Jo didn't want you to be compromised with the high council in any way. She said that you had enough trouble with them and didn't need more.'

Mari briefly closed her eyes. Jo had been so wrong. It didn't matter to her what a person looked like or where they came from. She had run the only refuge in the whole city. It had been necessary to dispense with all the classifications. When she opened them again she found all brothers facing the room in front of them. Before she could step back for privacy again they caught sight of an elder approaching them. 'Marianna. Mr. Jackson.' Elder Bryce sounded as if she had been moving quickly. Her half-moon glasses were sliding down her nose and her perfect silver bun was now slightly askew, 'I'm sorry for the delay but they're ready for you again.' 'One moment please Elder Bryce.' Scott had found himself impressed with the warriors who had been protecting them while they had been back in the city. He turned to the guard that silently reformed around them. 'If you need a place to go for a fresh start outside the city Jo has our com info. We will have jobs waiting for you.' He held his arm out to Marianna who silently slipped her hand into position resting lightly on his arm.

As they made their way back to the council chamber Mari could see that the unrest had begun to spread through the city. The children were being ushered through the tunnels back to the building that housed them when they weren't in training. She was sure that the children would be in held in lock down. She lowered her eyes and followed Elder Bryce back into the council chamber.

Their personal guard took up post around them as they were seated in front of the high council. Mari clasped her hands loosely in her lap and waited to hear their decision. She could not help but let her eyes wander to the spot where John's body had been twisted and broken. He had been alive when they had moved him from the room. She was sure of it. She could still feel his black anger swirling around the council chamber. She shivered. Scott looked at her. Mari could see concern in his eyes. Madame Speaker rose.

'Marianna de Montmercy and Mr. Scott Jackson we find your contract valid and reasonable in light of very recent occurrences. Go and be at peace with our blessings.'

'Thank you my lady. Will the high council permit me to leave as soon as my business in Spark City is concluded?' Mari asked her smile conveying real joy to them.

'We wish you the joy of life.'

They waited until the high council filed out before leaving the inner chambers. It was complete chaos in the building and surrounding streets. Their silent guards escorted them as far as Mercy House before disappearing up a side alley. Once they were alone in the lift Scott pulled her into his arms. He held her gently knowing he needed to reassure himself that they were both alright. His fingers brushed her earlobes and found them bare of the earrings she had slipped in that morning.

'Mari,' he sounded slightly amused, 'what happened to your earrings?' She lifted her head off his chest with a completely in-

nocent look on her face, 'They went better with Jo's outfit.'
The elevator doors opened. Jo approached looking completely
ladylike in a deep purple chiffon dress. There was nothing out
of place and if he hadn't seen her earlier he could have sworn
she had a twin. In Jo's hands were the missing earrings without
the pearl centers. Mari raised her face to his, 'They made a nice
smoke screen didn t they?'

He asked directly into her ear, 'Smoke bomb earrings? I love
your diabolical mind.' She gave him a mischievous grin as
she accepted her earrings from her friend. 'I thought I mislaid
these.' She hugged Jo, 'Thank you for taking care of my small issue for me.' There were too many people on the business level
for her to be more direct. Jo pointed up and Mari nodded.

Once they were seated comfortably in the penthouse Jo asked,
'So now what? The High Council approved your courting.' Scott
had his arm around Mari's shoulders. He replied easily, 'We go
home. I don t find city life agrees with me.' Jo could appreciate
that. The city life wasn't even for people who came from the
city. Many children learnt this lesson the hard way out in the tenements. Scott looked through one of the large picture windows
as he said, 'I had a message from home this morning. The
storm season has already begun.'

'Do we need to travel light?' Mari was thinking of the bags she
had already packed. She looked around her former home. This
life seemed ostentatious to her now after spending time in the
territories. What she had considered everyday items they would
see as complete frivolity. 'Just show Jo what you want for the
house and come spring she can crate it up with your meds. The
bags at the apartment can come now.' Scott squeezed her hand
gently.

'You will want the Degas.' Jo pointed at the painting she had
caught Mari staring at whenever she was deep in thought. The
Monet too.' Mari added. Those two paintings had been a part
of the de Montmercy inheritance ever since her fifth foremother
had had the foresight to rescue them at auction right around

the time the world had come to a standstill. There was nothing more she would regret leaving behind except the female in front of her. She could foresee another fight between man and the high council brewing very soon. John had showed her that today with the disdain he had treated the system she had grown up under. The turmoil was still going on in the center of the city and Mari could see from her vantage point that they had finally called out the enforcers.

The laws of Anna were fast becoming obsolete and when the city turned on itself completely she didn't want to be caught up in the terrible fall out that would ultimately come with the rebellion that she knew was brewing. She had a bad feeling that Jo's brothers were somewhere at the heart of it.

She turned Jo and spoke quietly, 'I'm leaving you completely in charge of Mercy House. The heads of departments were sending so many reports that I was still doing my job from the territories. You have to be Lady Mercy now.' Jo opened her mouth but Mari held her hand up silencing her so she could continue, 'They need to learn to listen to you. They will respect you if you listen to their request and try to find a compromise so everyone is happy. Remember what Mercy House stands for. Focus on that and every other decision will be easy to make. Even dealing with the high council.'

'You're walking away completely then?' Jo struggled to make sense of what she was saying. 'Something's coming. I don't understand what it is yet. I have a feeling that there will be a rebellion soon.' Mari's reply was slightly cryptic. She added, 'I will always be a part of Mercy House. Just not so involved anymore. Take care of them Jo.'

Jo could respect her choices. It hadnt been working and Mari had been too far away. If rebellion was coming a change of director was essential so that they would survive. Mari's decision made instant sense. She dipped her head at her friend, 'Take care of you.'

Chapter Seventeen - The Way of the Eight

The train chugged to a standstill in the middle of the night. The snow covering the tracks had made them impassable. Scott stood in the doorway of the sleeping area. He had no choice but to wake Mari early. She had never experienced the extreme weather he was about to take her out into. He placed a mug of sweetened tea beside her before shaking her gently.   Scott watched as her silver eyes focussed on him.

'It's time.' He told her, 'The porter said they would begin unloading the storage cars as soon as possible.' The machinery would freeze solid if they waited too long to get moving again. The train would shunt its way back to Spark City and wait there until after the thaw. Mari sipped the tea slowly as she watched him pull her thermal clothing out of the closet. He had been watching for trouble. Scott still expected some form of retaliation from the Smythe family for their retribution at the high council.

Mari dressed quickly. She left her hair in its single braid as Scott swirled her cloak around her body and fastened it for her. They had prepared for the journey as best as they could in a city that had never dealt with the reality of nature. Most of their supplies had been left loaded on the wagon. They had been assured that the horses had been bred hardy enough to survive the cold.

Before they stepped outside Scott stopped her, 'Don't go wandering. You won't be able to see much and if you wander too far you will die before any help will come. Stay where I leave you.' At the look of trepidation on her face he added reassuringly, 'I won't be gone for too long.' He left her beside the steps they had just climbed down with the three bags they had taken into the suite with them.

Mari could easily see why he had warned her against wandering as it was hard to see the end of the train carriage they had been in from where she stood precariously leaning on her crutch. Jo had found her one made from a new design. It was like nothing she had ever seen before. The foot on it was a wider base with spiked tread covering the bottom.

The cold seeped into her clothing and Mari was thankful for all the layers that Scott had insisted upon. Even her cloak was made from the fur of an animal she couldnt identify. He had had the fashion rooms make it to his own specifications and it had been delivered with the rest of their clothing to her apartment.

Her breath spiraled out into the air in front of her. She could hear the noise of the other passengers slowly beginning to disembark. No one wanted to leave the warmth of the train. As the noise of the complaining rose up into the night sky the staff began offering the return trip back to the city at double the original price of the ticket. She stood silently watching as many handed over the asking price displaying relief as they climbed back aboard.

Scott stopped the covered wagon beside her and helped load the last of their bags in the back. They had most of their supplies stored up the sides of the wagon hanging by hooks in specific spots so that they would not confuse the bundles. There was a nest of furs and blankets on the bed of the wagon right behind the driver's seat. He settled her in them and made sure she was fully covered.

He had made sure she could see out from her sheltered position as they travelled. He wasn t sure if she suffered from travel sickness. His chosen had never said. *His chosen.* He smiled at the thought. The words sparked a warmth inside him that he had never felt before. Checking over his shoulder to make sure she was alright she offered him a small tremulous smile. Clicking softly to the horses he pulled them away from the machine that seemed alien in the night and the people whose basic instincts would soon take over once they realized they had not prepared well after all.

'Where are we?' Mari asked when all the noise they could hear was the horses hoof beats against the frozen ground. She could see as far as the circle of light ahead cast by the solar lights attached to the sides of the harnesses. 'We were maybe a day from Bordertown by train.' Scott converted the distances in his head, 'It will be two or three days by wagon as long as the passes hold.' He sounded as if it would be dangerous for them to be trapped in the mountainous area. She asked gently, 'How long do we have before that happens?'

'A month at best a few days at worst.' Came his cryptic reply. The sun was trying to shine through the heavy clouds bathing the whole landscape in an odd shade of pink. It was so odd that it was bordering on orange. Mari couldn't ever remember seeing that particular shade before and wished she could free her sketchbook so she could capture it down on paper. 'Is this natural?' She asked as she poked her head out beside Scott to see the whole landscape better. He kissed her briefly, 'It is a rare phenomenon whenever the clouds get too heavy for the sun to shine through. Get back under the furs and blankets until the day warms up properly.' He checked on her and added, 'We are in Eighters territory. You need to stay inside hidden from their view except for when we stop for a break.'

'Eighters? What are Eighters?' Mari asked. 'The way of the Eight. ' Scott clarified for her, 'They're a who. One of the tribes of males who for generations have lived their whole lives by stealing, raiding, killing and hurting females to benefit themselves. They obey the laws of Eight.' His voice had sounded so grim that she put the pieces together in her head. She sounded confused as she spoke, 'If they're such a threat why have I never heard of them before?'

'Because they followed the rules that governed the territories before our forefathers heard of Anna. This is a splinter group that continue to live by the old ways shunning the laws of Anna completely. They have spies posted throughout the woods and mountains in case something good comes their way'. He let her process the new information before continuing, 'John mentioned the Eight when we were in the high council. The males guarding us were Eighters. They bore the infinity tattoo behind their left ear.'

Mari looked at him horror on her face. 'They will know of us already then.' Her voice was as icy as the wind that howled through the trees. 'No one knows what their tech capabilities are. It is very possible that they do not and we may be able to sneak through their territory without provoking a confrontation. It is best not to underestimate them.' Scott admitted to her, 'They have only used swords in the past but knowing John Smythe they may have better tech now.

Susanna was almost taken by them four winters ago.' His words were enough to silence the thoughts swirling through her mind. 'How?' the word seemed to barely float above the stillness of their surroundings. She watched Scott scan the tree line around them before he said quietly, 'They dropped from the trees and cut through the canopy.' They had to get out of the forest. His father had said that the wild males had dropped from the trees and cut open the wagon canopy to get to Susanna. They had almost lost her four winters ago because he had underestimated the Eighters brute strength and the lengths they had been willing to go to for a new female.

Nick had tracked Susanna to the Eighters temporary camp halfway through the cave system deep within the mountains themselves. She had been tied up in a compromising position along with the other females who had been taken. Scott had not been told anything more beyond the fact that Nick had rescued her and brought her home to heal. He shook his head.

It was the reason he had had the wagon reinforced before agreeing to buy it. Scott had had the engineer design a cage structure with a trapdoor in the wagon bed itself. Mari had assumed he had added the structure for the extra hanging space to give them more room in the wagon bed. Now he had to hope that it would be enough to help keep her safe.

He had lost count of the times Nick and Susanna had made the trip to the city too late in the season to return the whole way by train. Every time they returned home by wagon his dad warned him of the dangers and let him know of any land mark changes just in case he too one day would have to make the same trip. The biggest warning Nick always gave was 'Never put your female in danger that could have been avoided.' It had been a lesson branded deep into his soul.

The Eighters were true backwoods males living only on what they could hunt and what they could steal. Scott had dealt with them a few times trading supplies for information and he was thankful Mari had to hide under the bulky cloak to stay warm. He looked up at the mountain range they still had yet to cross. He had done it before on horse and it hadnt been easy then. He didnt expect it to be any easier now especially with the weather against them.

The light had changed from that odd shade of pink/orange to mid-morning sun filtering through the leaves. It bathed the frozen forest around them in golden light. Both horses tossed their heads as they easily cantered along the path that ran beside the train tracks. As they came to an open clearing Scott stopped the wagon and poked his head back through the cover. Mari had been extremely quiet since he had warned her of the dangers ahead. 'Ready to stretch your legs?' he asked interrupting her sketching of what looked like new weaponry.

She met him at the back of the wagon clutching the handle of her crutch tightly in her hand. 'It's so pretty here.' She said in wonder as he joined her after checking the horses. 'Pretty but still deadly. We can explore the snow more when we get to Bordertown.' He made sure the deep hood of her light brown cloak covered her hair completely, 'The Eighters use this trail all the time. Its best to keep moving.'

Mari thought about his words before commenting,'They didnt bother the train.' He helped support her over a slippery patch of ice before replying,'They have in the past. It's best not to tempt a starving frozen man with things that aren't his.' He bent his head and gave her a quick kiss before resuming their walk.

They had walked a full circle around the clearing back to the wagon when Scott warned her,'The Eighters are a law unto themselves. They listen to no one but their chief. If they come, we will have no option but to fight'. She heard his words and the meaning behind his words. They would kill him and take her. She needed to go through the weaponry they had on hand to be ready for an attack. Scott stood guard as she took care of her pressing personal needs and when she was ready he helped her back into the wagon. He locked the cage door behind her making sure it was secure.

He hated to lock her in but she would need to learn to trust his instincts more if they were to get to Bordertown in one piece. He had no doubt she was inside checking and double checking that their weapons were ready to use at a moment's notice. He had trusted her implicitly in the city and he would keep doing so. Now he needed to take lead and she needed to let him. Scott checked the horses again making sure that they were fresh enough for another few hours before quickly disappearing to do his business behind the same tree. He hoped that masking her scent with his they would be able to keep the Eight off their trail long enough to get over the mountains.

Mari had settled down into the furs and blankets. He took a

look over his shoulder after climbing back into the seat in front of her. She had taken some parts from one of the bundles and was concentrating on the project in front of her. He could see a piece of pipe from a folding walking stick and her knock out hair pins. 'New weapon?' Scott asked warily. He recognized the same look she had had on her face when she had been trying to figure out her walking stick bombs.

'Blow dart and pipe.' She answered as she assembled the weapon in front of him with ease. She packed away the spare parts into the bundle hanging closest to her before asking, 'What are the main differences between the laws of the Way of the Eight and Anna's laws?' Knowledge wasn t just wisdom. Knowledge of one 's enemy was a weapon to be used against them if needed.

Mari made herself comfortable as Scott spoke, 'The legend goes that the Way of the Eight was based on Bushido. Bushido was an honor code used in the ancient world by great warriors. The eight morals they focused upon were justice, courage, mercy, politeness, sincerity, honor, loyalty and self-control of character. All males aspired to attain all eight aspects of the code to the best of their abilities. When Anna's laws came to the territories the elders incorporated these morals and added rules about the specific way a female was to be treated.' He stopped for a moment to listen to their surroundings.

Satisfied they were still alone Scott continued, 'Anna's laws are more rules forcing people to live a certain way. The world before us took everything for granted. We bred ourselves nearly out of extinction. No one can say whether Anna's laws or the Way of the Eight are completely perfect. My forefathers had a saying. All a person can do is live the best way they know how under the system that is currently in place.'

'The Eighters don t seem to be following their own honor code now.' She commented. Scott privately agreed. There was change coming to the mountains as well as the cities. 'Something is definitely changing in this territory and I don t like it.' He spoke thoughtfully. Mari's questions were similar to the ones he had asked Susanna about the contract and Anna's laws not long after Mari had arrived on the farm. Susanna had expressed a personal belief that every territory and city seemed to have ancient beliefs incorporated into the laws of Anna which was why they were still diverse enough to have separate cultures.

He wasn t sure if he would be able to keep his family out of the storm. Scott knew one thing though and that was they were strongest when they were together. He looked over his shoulder to find Mari asleep. She would need all the rest she could get if it came to a hand to hand fight. Once they were out of immediate danger he would teach her how to drive the wagon. She couldn't stay hidden the whole way back to the farm.

During their next stop Mari learnt how to start a stew over a camp fire and then pack it in a foam box to keep cooking. They made enough food for them to keep travelling all day and well into the night without any more stops. Mari felt more than a little unsettled. She was used to the subtle politics and overt power plays of the city. 'They hunt us as if we are animals.' She spoke quietly breaking the silence.

'Not for much longer. They re in the tree line just watching us.' Scott replied keeping his tone light as if they were having a normal conversation. Mari sat just inside the wagon out of sight of everyone but Scott as he drank his cup of coffee. 'Why aren't they attacking?' she asked matching his tone evenly. He took another mouthful of his coffee and swallowed before answering, 'They like to learn any weaknesses we may have before coming down out of the trees. Dad thinks that they ve spent the last ten years gathering data on people travelling around the territories.' He covertly moved his gun closer to her. Mari flashed him the sight of a throwing knife tucked into her sleeve.

Mari studied him with undisguised curiosity. Reading his menacing body language, she knew that he was expecting an attack any minute. Gone was the man who had relied on her knowledge of the enemy for the last week. In his place was the dangerous confident man she had first been introduced to. 'Stand in the exact center of the wagon.' Scott spoke without looking at her, 'Get your weapons. Go now.' She moved without hesitation.

Chapter Eighteen - The Cave

Soft birdcalls punctuated the air from all directions. Scott continued to monitor them as he calmly continued to drink the cup of coffee Mari had made him. He could tell by the moving bird calls that they were surrounded. He heard the horses neighing. They too felt threatened by the shadows that moved in and out of their peripheral vision. He knew the attack would come swiftly once the animal sounds faded.

Mari concentrated on keeping her core muscles stable. She had to use all the balance she could muster. She stroked the handle of one of her throwing knives in front of her. She was sure that the Eighters were using the suspense of an attack as a way to throw them off balance. The forest around them erupted in a chilling war cry. It skittered all the way down her spine and in the dead silence that immediately followed she heard Scott's warning, 'Maybe six. Maybe more. Concentrate on protecting the horses.'

Mari loaded her improvised dart gun and stood watching completely motionless. There was movement in her line of sight. She kept her position waiting until they had their hands on the

horses harnesses. She could see that the males had camouflaged themselves in white to blend in with the snow. She
picked them off in rapid succession. Unwilling to use up all her
hair pins she scooped up a handful of her throwing knives off
the top of a barrel. She had lain her weapons out in preparation.

Maybe they were used to kidnapping females from the cities
who had only been trained in the ways of pleasure. She wasn't
their usual target and they weren't going to take her chosen
from her either. She flicked two knives towards the horses with
a practiced hand. Two bodies fell with a soft thud. Her focus
swung to the back of the wagon in time to see Scott pick up an
Eighter weapon to fight with.

She knew that there was an Eighter in the wagon with her but
she needed to know that he was still alright. She pretended to
be distracted right up until she could feel his fetid breath on her
neck. 'Haven't you heard of fresh breath?' she asked as she
nicked him with one of her blades. She watched him stumble
twice before kicking him off the back of the wagon with a good
kick to his rear. She flicked another two knives toward the front
opening and kept throwing them intermittently.

Scott forced his opponent around near the horses. It was the
first time he had seen an Eighter up close. He took note of the
man's stylized fighting moves that resembled the warriors of
old that their belief system had been based in. Contrary to the
common held belief that they were true mountain men he was
neatly dressed in what looked like a well-kept uniform.

They fought in a wide circle around the wagon. As they passed
around the horses Scott parried each blow with ease. She
had dropped seven bodies. Each one had one of her throwing
knives buried in the exact same place in their bodies. He was
glad that she was fighting with him. It took skill to place a knife
in the same spot in the heat of a battle. He kicked his opponent
back around the tail end of the wagon only to see a throwing
knife bury itself deep in the Eighter's chest. He went down with

a surprised gurgle. Blood spilled from his lips in a thin stream.

Mari appeared in the opening of the wagon. Scott was scanning the trees for a second wave when she spoke, 'Are there any more? He shook his head and as he bent down to retrieve her knife she spoke quickly, 'Don t touch the blade. I dipped them in poison. The tiniest cut is all it will take for you to look like him.' The Eighter had swollen up and his skin was turning a nasty shade of purple.

'Consider your warning well received. Go collect your weapons. We leave nothing of ourselves behind.' He looked up at the sky thanking the many gods of creation for her deadly aim. He cleaned his sword of the blood and gore before moving from beside the corpse.

Mari navigated the snow and ice as best as she could on her own. The streaks of blood from where the dead men had dragged themselves for the last few seconds of their lives were stark against the landscape. He joined her and silently gave her the knife she had thrown out the back of the wagon. 'Can I have one of their swords?' She asked as they finished the delicate job of removing her knives and knockout pins. She was pleased to see that they still had a half dosage remaining in each of them.

Scott passed one to her and kissed her before moving away to start checking on the horses for injuries. 'What do you want with it?' She tipped her head on its side as she studied the weapon she held in her hands. It was well made and finely balanced. She couldn't see any buttons or catches in the hilt and couldn't identify the metal that it was made out of.

It felt like an extension of her body as she tried a sweeping figure eight in the air. Even more perplexing was its lack of weight compared to its size. 'They're studying us. I want to know this weapon and I want to know if I can modify it to give us an advantage if they attack again.' She looked at him, 'The ones that do wake up will have stories to tell.'

That made a lot of sense to him and as he settled back in the driver's seat he heard her mutter, 'What the hell is this stuff made of?' Scott hid a smile and looked up checking the position of the sun. They would need to find shelter soon for the night. He couldn't figure out why she had taken her eyes off the front of the wagon. 'Why did the Eighter get so close to you?' Thinking of the gamut of emotions that had run through him in those few heartbeats he was angry she had put herself in danger.

'I didn t know you saw that. I was worried about you.' Her face hadn't fully regained its color yet, 'You had me safe inside the wagon. I wanted to make sure you were alright.' Scott nodded his head at her explanation. It made sense to him on an emotional level. 'Next time I tell you to do something it's because I want to keep you safe as well.'

He looked up at the sky trying to think of a way to put what he was feeling into words. Mari filled the silence for him. 'I could have been the distraction that could have cost you your life.' She curled up under the furs as tight as her clothing would allow. 'You could have.' He didn t the energy to sugar coat words for her, 'This time we were lucky. Don t take such a risk again.'

Light was fading as Scott found the cave he had been hunting for at the base of the mountains. It was a confusing network of caves and tunnels that he had stumbled across during his years of aimless wandering. He guided the horses through to the second cave that he had set up as a vehicle area. He was pleased to see that the temporary horse stall was still there and someone had left behind some feed as well.

He helped Mari down from the back of the wagon and led her through the maze to stand in the darkness while he lit an old light in the center of the last cave they came to. It was as he remembered spacious with that cozy feeling. He watched as she removed her heavy hooded cloak.

Laying it over the end of the sleeping platform she began to explore her new surroundings. The area was wreathed in shadows at the edges of the circle of light. Mari looked ethereal in the flickering light. Scott cleared his throat as he dropped an armload of furs and blankets on the sleeping platform. He tossed the bag off his back onto the floor. 'I'll take care of the horses. We should be safe here tonight.'

While waiting Mari made the sleeping platform and organized their supplies. Once finished the mundane chores she trailed her fingers in the bathing pool in the corner. The water was warm and felt amazing against the back of her hand. She wondered how the water managed to stay at such a constant temperature without overheating or losing its temperature. She felt the gaps in her knowledge keenly when she came across something new and couldn't understand how it worked.

'Why don't you get in.' Scott had returned. He was leaning against the wall of the cave with an unreadable expression on his face. He had watched her delight at the touch of the cave walls and her perplexed look as she rubbed the dirt of the floor through two of her fingers and her thumb. He had seen the brief sadness as it flashed across her face a few seconds ago followed by her mask of calm acceptance that he had grown to hate. He had seen the look of pure joy as she dipped her hand in the water. He wanted to see more of that emotion on her face.

She removed her boots then turned her back to him. As she undressed she dropped each article of clothing in a pile beside her. She raised her hands to her head and pulled out the hairpins slowly. Her fingers moving through her hair with surety as lastly she uncoiled and unbraided her hair. Her tresses fell around her shoulders in soft waves and down her back to hide the scars.

She dipped a foot in the water the same way she had been playing with it with her hand. Mari looked over her shoulder at Scott, 'why don't you join me?' He watched as she slipped under the water and reappeared a few seconds later. She allowed him his privacy as she found a natural rock formation she could comfortably sit on and soak the pain out of her bad leg near the edge of the pool. She could hear the rustling of clothing being removed and the clank of his weapons belt hitting the floor.

Mari closed her eyes as the heat of the water started to relax her sore muscles. 'Beautiful.' He spoke in her ear. She hadn't heard him walk across the floor and she turned her head to meet his kiss. She stopped paying attention to everything but the feel of his lips against hers. His tongue slid into her mouth and as he stroked it against her own she let out a moan of pleasure.

Sometime later when the world had stopped spinning he realized she was still draped across his chest quietly listening to his heartbeat. She raised her head to look at him. 'Siren.' He ran a hand down the side of her face. Her grey eyes were tranquil and he realized that this was the first time he had seen her truly relaxed. 'Are you ok?' She asked as he began to play with her hair winding wet strands around his finger. 'Are you?' At her nod he kissed her forehead then added, 'We're going to do that again but first we need food.'

The stew that they had started earlier that day tasted delicious. Mari realized she was not limping as badly as she normally did. Her muscles must have relaxed during her soak. As she pushed her half dry locks over her shoulder for the fifth time while going through their food supplies looking for their breakfast Scott patted a spot in front of him on the sleeping platform. 'Let me give you a hand combing out your hair.' He offered when she finally located the item she had been looking for.

She found her comb and as he worked she quietly drew in her sketch pad in front of him. Once he had gathered all her hair and braided it for her he leaned over her shoulder to see the cave around them depicted on the sketch pad. The drawing was so life like he could have sworn that he could hear the stew bubbling over the fire. She closed the book and put it down beside their bags when he started to gently rub her back.

He was running his fingers lightly over her scars on her back as if he could trace them away. 'Some ancient warriors used to scar their bodies whenever they passed tests requiring immense courage and skill.' He kissed her shoulder, 'These tell the story of a warrior so great that no male can ever hope to match her in battle.' Mari raised her head so she could look him in the eyes, 'There are many different ways to engage in a battle. All I did was merely survive mine.' He drew her down with him into the nest of furs and blankets.

They listened to the wood popping and crackling in the fire pit for a while before Mari roused herself enough to ask another question, 'Will they come after us again tomorrow?' Scott was drawing distracting circles on her stomach with his forefinger. 'We are likely to have a skirmish with them once a day now until we reach the edge of their territory.' He raised himself up on one elbow as she rolled onto her back, 'We did leave some of them alive. You aren't going to be safe until we get into Border-town.'

He dropped a kiss on the end of her nose just to hear her laugh. She grew serious again. 'I'm not going to hide if you get overrun by Eighters. We were only playing with them and they know it. Next time they will send more men.' Scott's expression mirrored hers, 'Not only will you hide, you will escape through the trap door in the wagon bed because I will lock you in the cage and let the horses go.' He watched the emotions dance across her face.

Caging. It had been a key point in the contract for a reason. She couldn't even form the words at the horrific thought of being caged right before he expected her just to leave him behind. She knew that she had made a mistake in trying to watch his back as well as her own.

She rolled toward him and buried her face in his chest. He stroked her hair, 'We fight together. You watch my back from the shadows. They won't get their hands on you. The cage is our last option.' He felt her nod her head. He knew that she wasn't afraid to fight. She wouldn't leave him to die for her without coming back for him. It just wasn't part of who she was. Scott held Mari until he could hear her breathing slow down. He wished he could explain to her just what she would be facing if she were captured. Susanna had never shared any of it with him and when he had asked his dad he had turned away with a haunted look in his eyes.

'Mari?' He pulled back a little so he could see her face. Her expression was solemn and her eyes were huge. 'You are precious to me.' He admitted. The pretty words he had once used in days gone by were stuck in his throat and he hoped she understood that his feelings ran deep. 'You are precious to me as well.' She replied softly. He framed her face with his hands and kissed her before adding, 'Then you understand that this cage is temporary for your safety. I don't even want to think about what they do to their females. What they would do to you.'

She nodded knowing he could feel it with his hands still around her head. He folded her back in his arms so she could hear his heartbeat as she fell asleep. 'I trust you.' Her whisper floated to his ears just as he had almost completely relaxed.

Chapter Nineteen - Compassion

Scott was struggling to find the wheel ruts he had been following the day before. A significant amount of snow had fallen overnight. The world was almost eerily silent around them as they started the long climb high into the mountains. He had studied the mountain range from the mouth of the cave only that morning. He had contemplated leaving the wagon at the base of the range and loading up one of the horses with their essentials.

He had seen Mari attempt riding on the farm and discarded that plan with a grin. Able horsewoman she was not. Scott was not regretting the gentle climb he had chosen that switched back and forth on itself. Mari would not realise how high they really were until they crested one of the peaks overlooking the valley.

The weather had been building for most of the morning and he was keeping an eye on the colour of the clouds. More snow would hamper their travelling soon and he didn t want to be caught outside in the open when the next ice storm hit.

Mari shivered and huddled in on herself even further. She was bundled inside her heavy ankle length cloak and their bedding again. Scott had insisted that she put on extra layers of clothing to keep her warm that morning and she hadn't argued but even they didn't seem to be helping against the severe cold. She knew Scott was checking on her periodically. She didn't have the energy to try to reassure him that she was alright. Her eyes met his with a silent plea to find shelter fast.

She knew that it was dangerous to stay in one cave network for any more than a couple of nights. They had been careful not to leave a trail behind them however she had found fresh boot prints in the snow outside of the cave they had just spent the night in. The Eighters had picked up their trail again. Scott didn't know from the prints exactly where the Eighters were. It had been enough for them to immediately pack and move further up the trail.

The truth of how miserable Mari was truly feeling was written across her face. Scott knew the conditions were becoming more treacherous for her every time they ventured out into the cold on two feet. Mari's health and comfort was a real concern in his mind. He was hunting for the next cave where she could warm up and thaw out in. He knew that if they didn't keep moving fast enough the high passes would close and they would be stuck in the Eighters territory until the next warm season. They would run short of supplies and lose the animals as well. The storms in this area tended to roll in on top of each other.

Scott was so deep in thought that he almost missed it. There. An entry to a cave. It was barely visible through the sheets of diagonally falling snow but he directed the horses straight at it. When he stopped the wagon he noticed that there were two horses already bedded down for the rest of the day and without a word Scott slipped down from the wagon to scout who was in residence. Mari struggled up out of the bedding. The pain in her leg had grown so bad that she was having trouble walking with any kind of normalcy.

She gathered the supplies they would need for the night and possible day ahead. Scott appeared quickly in front of her and grabbed the healing bag they kept at the back of the wagon on a low hook, 'There's sick people back there.' He helped her down and added, 'Any trouble and don't hesitate to use a knock out hairpin on them.' Mari could deal with the sick better than the cold. She nodded her head in agreement and mentally prepared herself for anything.

Scott led her to a cave similar to the one they had shared the previous night. The couple were lying on a sleeping platform in filth encrusted blankets. The cave was warm and there was a pot suspended over the fire. Mari's gaze continued around the cave noticing another thermal pool and the pitiful amount of food stores stacked against one wall neatly. She glanced quickly in the pot only to find a thin broth. One of them must have made the effort to keep fresh food going that day she concluded.

Mari moved closer to the couple pushing the deep hood off her braid as she drew near. They looked to be younger than her by five or six seasons. The female had deep purple hair shorn short with pale skin and cracked lips. The male had black hair and mating tattoos. The way he had wrapped the female up Mari couldn't tell if she had the matching tattoos. She crouched painfully down by the female and touched a hand to each forehead in turn. Hot and dry. She looked up at Scott, 'I need light.'

She checked their pulse while she was waiting and leaned back on her heels thinking. His was strong. Her's was weak and intermittent. Scott returned with the light and watched as she pulled up their eyelids to check their pupils and their lower lids down. The female's cheeks were red. The man was awake watching her touch the female with care.

'Tia. My mate. Help her.' even those few words seemed to be a struggle as he begged for her to help the female. Mari touched his hand briefly then looked up at Scott, 'I think they both need fluids and food. I can't be sure what it is until you've cleaned him up some. Look for puncture marks and rashes.' She turned back to the male, 'I will do what I can for you both.' She tried to reassure him but with only a basic knowledge of physical healing she didn't think Tia would survive any more than the next couple of hours. Scott handed her a mug of broth and she fed a few sips to the male. Mari checked Tia again and raised her eyes to Scott, 'Can you help him in the pool please?'

She rose unsteadily and made her way over to the bench in front of the fire pit. Removing her jacket and rolling up her sleeves she laid out the contents of the bag in front of her while thinking about the symptoms she was dealing with. Tia was dreadfully hot and dry. She was afraid if they couldn't break the fever fast they would lose her. Snow. They had snow. Considering the small packages of healing herbs, she had packed for the journey Mari separated the white willow bark out of the pile and some crushed garlic cloves. Not bothering with her cloak she picked up their pail and left to get some snow from the entrance. Slowly working she stripped the female of her clothes and covered her with a sheet. After a couple of trips Scott silently took over gathering the snow and ice for her.

The male was watching from where Scott had laid him back down. His face was full of anguish and exhaustion. Mari gently rearranged Tia so he could hold her hand. She fed him some more of the broth before speaking gently and calmly, 'Her fever is very bad. If I cannot break it soon she may not survive this illness. It is time to make your peace with her I think.' She rose carefully and went back to the fire to make some white willow bark tea. Scott joined her so the young male could have the privacy he needed to say goodbye.

Scott watched as she made enough of the tea for them all and raised an eyebrow when she handed him one. 'A precaution. She said and began to make some honey water using their own supplies to do so. 'His name is Liam Hart and he's a mating tattooist. He knew his mate was sick when they came through Bordertown but he thought that he could get all the way to Spark City before he would need to take her to a healing center. They got caught in the white out day before yesterday and she's been getting worse ever since.' He watched her sip her tea. She leaned her head on his shoulder and closed her eyes.

Tia was fighting for her life. Each breath in seemed to be a monumental struggle. Mari wanted to believe that she would get better but she wasn't sure that she had the right herbs to help her. She sipped her tea again and continued to search her memory for any information she could use to help the sick couple. Anything she could think of only applied to the mildly sick. She rose to check Tia again and her brow creased as she realized that they were fighting a losing battle.

Scott crouched down beside her and watched as she attempted to get her to take more fluids. Mari asked softly, 'Have you been around this illness before?' It had swept through the city once when she had been much younger. Many had died especially in the rim tenements where personal hygiene was not as highly regarded. One out of every three females in the city's training dormitories had died and the high council had sealed the city to quarantine them from any more germs. Mari had caught it from the house staff. She had spent the next two weeks floating in and out of consciousness hearing snippets of conversations held over her. She finished what she was doing and looked at Scott in concern. He wasn't displaying any of the visible signs of what some elders had called 'the flu'.

Scott replied in the most reassuring tone he could muster, 'I've seen this before and survived.' His birth mother hadn't. He had only been young when one of the farm hands had come back from Bordertown sneezing. His mother had checked on him more than once and within a week she too had been flushed with fever. He would not risk bringing the illness back to the farm a second time. He looked at the couple and spoke again in a low voice, 'We have to leave when this storm finishes. If they survive the night, we will take them with us.' He could make up another bed in the back of the wagon.

He watched as Mari painstakingly fed Tia more honey water and after each mouthful massaging her throat to encourage her to swallow. He knew she was doing everything she could to convince the female's body not to give up. He wasn't sure that there was much else that they could do for her. He looked at the cave mouth. This was nothing like the cave networks he had been finding for them to hide in. He knew that they were still too exposed to both the elements and the ever present threat of the Eighters.

Scott had found the identification scar of the Eighters on Liam's shoulder when he had been tending to his needs. Neither male had spoken of the faint scar and it had been heavily tattooed over by one of Liams mating marks. He knew that Eighters would rather die than disrespect their tribal scars. It was one of the few pieces of cultural knowledge about the group that he knew. He watched as Mari limped over to check Liam again. When her attention was elsewhere he furtively checked the back of Tia's shoulder as well.

She had the same heavily tattooed over scar as part of her mating marks. Only her scar seemed to have been made with a branding iron. It was another part of the ongoing puzzle about the Eighters that didnt make any sense to him. Liam had chosen blackbirds as their symbol and both of the couple had one perched over their scar. Liam had inked Tia's marks with a grace and delicacy that made Scott feel as if they were a part of her beauty rather than a symbol of their long term attachment.

He lowered her back down gently then packed more snow on and around the soaking sheet that covered her. He laid her hand back in Liam's and almost held his breath as she opened her eyes. Using more energy than she had to spare she turned her head towards her mate as he squeezed her hand to let her know where he was. Scott faded back into the shadows a little and watched as Mari did the same on the other side of the sleeping platform. He knew that they were intruding on an intensely private moment.

The couple were so focused on each other that the world outside their small circle of light did not exist. 'Liam?' Tia's voice reminded Mari of a vibrant songbird. The effort it took to speak showed on her face and a tear rolled down her cheek of its own volition. She wanted more time. She wanted more for Liam. Tia tried to lift one of her hands but her body would not obey her demands.

At the sound of her voice Liam's face brightened. His expression betrayed none of the anguish he was feeling. He had not thought she would even wake again for him to tell her that he loved her. 'Not going anywhere.' He swallowed painfully. His eyes were memorizing every line of her face. 'Live.' Her voice was just loud enough for both Scott and Mari to hear. He was quiet as he processed what she had told him encompassed in that single word. Scott appeared from the shadows and scooped Tia up gently. He repositioned them together with her tucked under Liam's arm with her head on his chest. Scott exchanged a brief look of shared grief with Liam and then faded back into the shadows to wipe the tears from Mari's face.

It was painfully obvious to Mari that Tia didn t want to leave her mate and her heart broke for the couple lying in front of her. She felt Scott wrap both of his arms around her as they kept their silence. Liam rubbed Tia s hand soothingly and spoke in a calm voice, 'Close your eyes for me Christiana. Dream of the time we spent exploring the world together. Think of me when you ride the wind in the night. Never forget you are my heart.' His voice cracked slightly.

His face reflected his deep emotional turmoil and he was grateful that his beautiful mate could not see his pain. Liam was aware of the moment when Tia's eyes slid shut again but he kept rubbing her hand with slow circular motions. A few minutes later she let out a rattling breath and then lay silent.

Mari waited for five minutes before coming forward to lay two fingers against Tia's neck. There was no longer any throbbing in the vein. She could feel Liam's eyes on her as she slowly moved her hand away. Looking up to meet his eyes she gently shook her head. She watched him with concern as his eyes slid shut, his hand relaxed in Tia's and he passed out. She moved over to check his vitals as Scott moved Tia's body against the cave wall and covered it with the sheet. Mari tugged Liam s blankets back up around his shoulders before touching his forehead briefly.

He would recover in time. Her heart bled for him.

Scott helped her back to the fire slowly where he poured her another cup of healing tea. She had fought long and hard to save the dying female before thinking of her own comfort. He took a look at her fingertips and hands before beginning a massage on the lower half of her bad leg. 'Rest for a few minutes.' He looked over at the motionless male, 'He will not be wanting anything for a while now.'

Later Mari checked Liams vitals again and fed him another cup of broth. She brushed his dark hair off his brow before joining Scott in their sleeping furs. 'I think his body has shut own involuntarily. The loss of his mate on top of his illness was too much for him to bear.' He wrapped his arms around her and let her listen to his heartbeat. He felt her tears as they dropped onto his bare chest. 'What do we do with Tia's shell?' she asked after a while. 'Body.' Scott automatically corrected her, We call the shell a body even after death.' He kissed behind her ear, 'Tomorrow I'll build a pyre and before we leave I'll light it. I do not know Liam's customs. This is the way of my forefathers.'

'Why do you burn the body?' He was not surprised by her innocent question. Every tribe and city seemed to have their own way of dealing with the dead and explaining away the afterlife. 'I will respect Christiana's body by purifying it with smoke as it turns to ash. My forefathers believed that we come from dust and we will return to dust. It's how you live your life in between that counts.' Scott rubbed her back absentmindedly.

Mari had been too busy surviving her life to question her beliefs before. Scotts answers had come from a personal level. In contrast, Spark City had a very rigid procedural way of dealing with the dead and those left behind. Once a person passed away the health department would usually come by for the shell and within the hour all the paperwork would be lodged for the family. The next call would be from the family lawyer so that all assets could be dispersed.

Mari hadnt questioned the practices before. The city had rhythms to it that now seemed cold and extremely heartless.

Tia had been a living person who had loved her mate deeply. Mari couldnt imagine surrendering her body to the health department never to see it again. She couldnt imagine forgetting she had ever existed. 'What's going through your pretty head?' Scott's lips touched her ear. 'Death customs.' She answered absentmindedly and then looked up at him, 'I come from a place where the authorities remove the shell from the premises as soon as the person has passed. I never thought about whether they treated someone with such respect, honour and dignity before.' A thought suddenly hit her. It would be an easy way for a person to disappear if they didn't want to be found again. She slipped into an uneasy sleep full of shadows and half memories.

Scott found her huddled in front of the fire drinking tea in the early hours of the morning. She was dressed in her heavy cloak and had all their weapons spread out in front of her. 'Need a hand?' he crouched down beside her. Her hair was loose around her shoulders and she was creating weapon designs that combined all the weapons spread out in front of her to make something even more deadly.

'I couldn't sleep.' She indicated her tea, 'Want one?' He tipped her chin up so he could see her face. 'I heard your screaming. All this is because of something more than the Eighters.' She briefly closed her eyes. When she opened them again she could still see the concern and something more than tenderness on his face. 'They told me Elanna was dead murdered by John. I never saw the body. My nightmares were of the day she handed me over to him. I still get them every once in a while. This is how I cope with the aftermath. I'm sorry I woke you up.' His eyes softened even further, 'You're here with me. Safe. I'm not going to let anything happen to you. Just like you're not going to let anything happen to me.' He helped her stand up and removed her outer garment.

'Come back to bed with me.' He watched her get into the furs and made sure they were both covered before making sure she could see his face. 'Nightmares are nothing to be ashamed of. From now on we discuss them rather than let our fears guide our actions.' He held her until he could see her slowly nod her head in agreement. He waited until she slid back into a deep sleep before moving.

Scott looked at the ceiling of the cave. He had never seen anyone walk into a sick room and take complete charge like she had the day before. The complete sensitivity she had shown in knowing when to fade into the shadows for the couple to have their privacy had to be innate. It was obvious that her healing after her traumatic experience had been mostly physical. The emotional scars were still bleeding through into her dreams on rare days. He clasped her hand and waited for the morning.

Chapter Twenty - Liam

The past, present and future was compressed in front of me within the pages of a leather bound book. It called to me whenever it was time to reveal a crucial piece of information. It had called to me at the moment of Tia's passing. Soul sick from the loss of the one person who had understood me better than any other I had succumbed easily.

Surrounded by healing purple light I saw a distinct junction in the history of the human race. I was shown the same piece of information twice. One, where the female who had been tending us survived to live her life with her mate and a much darker fate in which she was enslaved by the Way of the Eight. My father would sire more children on her and use her until she had no more reserves of energy left to tap. He would have her use the earth until it could no longer sustain any life at all.

My father. He had never been a good leader. He had never truly been any kind of father either. His leadership had led the Way of the Eight into the kind of stagnation that rotted from the core. He had made a deal with a man whose heart was as black as the dead of night. In turn, he himself had become the same type of man with only glimmers of light left in him.

He had never paid me much attention until the day I had approached him with a deal to save Tia's life. She had come to mean much more to me than any of the females who passed through the camp. She had seen me. Known me. Given me words for what it was that I could do. She had said that I was a seer. It was my job to bear witness to events. To subtly guide them in a path best for humanity. It was my job to watch but not intervene unless the alternative was so great that the whole of humanity would be lost.

It seemed as if the day was coming where I could no longer travel from town to town bearing witness to many mated couples happiness. I would once again have to make a stand.

The light surrounding me was growing brighter. Almost burning me as it insisted that I be healed. Too much. The female was taking too much upon herself. I would not have the sharp grief that came with losing a mate. In her compassion, the female was expending too much of herself.

It seemed as if the female was untrained in the ways of using her innate abilities. Her male companion seemed not to notice either. Maybe where they came from discussing ones abilities was a taboo subject. It would surprise them to learn just how many differences there were.

My Tia had been a collector of such pieces of knowledge. If there were even whispers of a new talent revealing itself in any town we were staying in she would ask the right subtle questions until she had enough information to scribble down in her book. Her book. She had brought it with her into the camp. Most of the males in the Eight were good with a sword or a bow. Words on a page eluded them. Her book had made its way into my hands and from my hands back to hers. One day her book would make its way into the hands of the fated female of the prophecy. The prophecy about the fall of the rule of the followers of the great Anna.

The light softened around me and consciousness once again beckoned. I didn t want to emerge back into the world without my Tia. I had no choice.

Chapter Twenty-One - Acceptance

Scott began to build the pyre as soon as the storm had blown past them. The wood had still been wet so he had had to use quite a lot of the stored firewood inside the cave. Mari had been watching as he chopped up a couple of already fallen trees to dry out before the next travellers came through the cave. She hadn't spoken of her nightmares again. He hadn't mentioned it. He was anxious to get underway as soon as possible. If Eighters knew they were so exposed, he had no doubts they would attack again without hesitation.

Inside Mari prepared Liam for travel. He had made it through the night but had not yet woken up. She used the opportunity to calm her thoughts. Her hands were slightly warmer as she continued to heal Liams body despite his mind shutting down temporarily. As she looked around the cave Mari realised that it would make Liam's life easier to have his own personal belongings with them as well.

A beam of sunlight finally broke through the clouds as Scott scooped up Tia's covered body. He laid her on the top of the pyre of logs and branches he had piled up. In the few seconds she had been lucid enough to greet her mate he had seen the gentle soul for who she was. The fire would alert every Eighter in the immediate area. He had no option but to light it otherwise hungry animals would desecrate her remains and her soul would be trapped forever wandering in a living world she could no longer be a part of.

Mari kept her hood up as she made numerous trips between the cave and the wagon Scott had moved outside. She could not help wonder if something larger was guiding their steps in this journey. Liam seemed to be starting to return to consciousness. His brow was beginning to crease with pain and she could see some rapid eye movement.

Whoosh. The wood caught alight rapidly as Scott lit it from one of the burning logs from the inside fire he had just doused. The red flames ate gleefully along the wood base before starting to lick along the support branches. Mari watched Scott make a strange ritualistic gesture with his fingers touching his forehead, lips and chest as if to say thank you to Tia for the privilege of knowing her even for such a short period of time.

As Mari turned she caught sight of Liam laid along the opposite side of the wagon from where she would be sitting. She could just make out his bearded face underneath all the spare blankets and furs they had managed to scavenge out of the cave for him. She knew that very soon he would have to face Tia's death and that her healing work with his mind would begin.

Scott had found a crossbow and arrows in the cave during their clean up. He'd given them to her to examine. Mari took the time to look with a keen gaze. She had found nothing abnormal about the bow at all. It was the arrows that interested her. The tips looked as if they had been handmade and dipped in something. The markings along the shaft were animalistic in nature almost like a stylized mating tattoo. Like the stylized tribal tattoo that seemed to cover Liam from the waist up. They peeked out of his neck line and down one arm. She carefully put them back in the small leather quiver. Mari suspected the unknown coating would kill and without an antidote handy she had no intention of experimenting with it any further.

Scott swung up into the driver's seat. 'Remember,' his face was serious as he turned around to look at her, 'stay out of sight. If the Eighters attack join the fight from inside the cage. If I have to lock you in and they get to the horses-go and dont look back. Remember that you are my heart dont take risks.' He waited until she nodded.

Mari had never heard that particular phrase before she had met Nick and Susanna. She had not asked what it meant because she had not wished to intrude on what had seemed like a private moment between Scott's parents. 'What does the phrase you are my heart mean?' She asked him once they were moving again, 'I've heard Nick say it to Susanna and Liam say to it Tia. It is not commonly used in the city.'

'It is means more than a chosen in a contract. More than somebody someone has forced upon you. More than even love itself. You are the one person that he would die for and the only person he would kill without question for. You are his everything.' Liam answered before Scott could his voice weak from lack of use and void of emotion, 'Most males only attribute such an attachment to their mates.' So much emotion encompassed in one little phrase. Mari knew she would be thinking it over when she had a chance.

Her silver eyes regarded Liam solemnly as she reached out to check his pulse and temperature again. 'Where's Tia?' He asked. His voice cracked slightly with undealt with emotions.

'I'm sorry Liam,' She said as gently as she could, 'Tia didn't make it. By the time I got to you both she was already slipping away.' His eyes glittered with unshed tears and she watched as he rolled towards the wall away from her. 'This is a nightmare made real.' She heard him say to the wall. She gripped his shoulder lightly in support before she dragged one of their furs towards herself and wrapped up in it. She remained quiet leaving him to come to terms with his mate's death. When he was ready to open up then she would be there to listen to him. His fever had finally broken and along with it his heart.

She spent the rest of the morning drawing her memory of Christiana curled up in Liam's arms. She didn't know if he would appreciate her having seen something so personal but she knew one day he would want the picture to remember her by. 'I failed her.'they were the first words he had spoken in hours. Mari stored her sketchbook and pencils carefully before answering in an even tone, 'You didn't fail her. When we arrived yesterday you begged us to take care of her first. It was you who kept her clean, fed and warm before we arrived. It was you who found shelter out of the storms and made sure the horses were cared for.'

'It wasn't enough.' Liam stared at the canopy of the wagon with grief etched in the features of his face. 'You couldn't have done more. The illness you have just had steals the lives of the strong, the weak, the young and the old. I have seen it before and it never discriminates.' Mari let him absorb her statement as she handed him a flask of white willow tea. She watched him sniff at the flask before acceptance washed over his face. He took a few large gulps and put the cap back on before he handed it back to her. She looked at the ice covered trees moving past the back of the wagon for a while until he said, 'You helped us without knowing who we were.'

'I did not know that we had to be introduced to help each other.' Mari said quietly, 'I'm Mari de Montmercy. My chosen is Scott Jackson. I didn't know your people or your customs. We meant no offense.' She had never had the policy of asking questions before rendering assistance. Did that matter to people in the territories she wondered as she stared at her hands in her lap. He had not known them either and yet he had still accepted her help with his mate.

Mari continued staring at her hands slightly for a few seconds before moving back to her usual spot behind the driver's seat near Scott. 'Did we do something offensive by helping Tia and Liam without asking their permission first?' 'No.' He spoke without turning his head, 'We're being watched again. Be ready. You remember what I told you?' Mari checked her weapons belt underneath her cloak.

'How much time do we have?' she asked in reply. 'Not long.' She could hear the concern in his voice. Mari raised her hood partially as she listened to the woods around them. Different breeds of owl were softly hooting from all directions. She could hear Liam pushing back his blankets. She turned to look in his direction only to see him rising from the bed they had made him. 'My bow.' The determined expression on his face forestalled any argument. 'On the wall above you along with your quiver and dagger.' Mari replied as she retrieved his boots and held them out to him.

'Where did you leave my Tia?' He asked looking up from his lacing. A quiet menace was beginning to emanate out of him. 'You don't have do this right now.' Mari replied as she made sure the wagonbed was completely clear of obstacles. Liam looked at her after checking his crossbow. He stepped right in front of her forcing her to meet his gaze, 'I must. The Eighters were my people once.' His face told her more than she needed to know. He had been in a fight of epic proportions and left everything he had known for Tia taking her with him.

Mari made a snap decision and answered him as gently as she could while preparing for a fight, 'We followed the ways of Scott's people. He built a pyre and said some words. I think the fire was meant to purify and release her spirit to fly free. We could not leave her body behind to be desecrated or worse for her to be trapped to wander the earth afraid.' Mari grabbed her walking stick bombs down off the wall and looked at him hard, 'You said these were once your people. Dont make me regret helping you.' Liam nodded once to let her know that he had understood her meaning as she limped to the center of the moving wagon.

Chapter Twenty-Two - Liam's family

Mari braced herself as Scott pulled the horses to a stop rather suddenly. The cacophony of noise invading the canopied space of the wagon was overwhelming. On top of the voices she could hear screeching at them there was a new sound. A frightening sound. A clanking sound. It sounded as if they were banging swords against shields in unison. They had to be outnumbered by at least a hundred males. 'Sound echoes here.' Liam spoke alleviating her thoughts somewhat. Scott turned locking the front door on the cage.

Mari could see a wave of humanity rushing at them from her view through the back of the wagon. She assumed that they were being assaulted from all sides. Twisting the handle of one of her sticks she hurtled it as hard as she could out over the tailgate. Liam dove out after it and slammed the back door shut locking her in the cage. The earth shook with a thunderous explosion. She witnessed the destruction her walking stick bomb had wrought as Scott yanked the canopy of the wagon off the cage.

He gave her a quick nod before moving to uncouple the horses.

Mari watched as they raced to the edge of the clearing only to be caught by the males who had them surrounded. Mari covered her hair properly. She clutched her blow dart pipe tightly in her grasp as she surveyed the scene outside the wagon. Scott was leaning against the cage calmly. His sword was in his right hand at the ready with his left hand resting on the butt of his gun. She continued to assess the situation and as she turned she realized the Eighters had massed around them.

By the looks on their faces she knew that they were furious with her. Her bomb had more than effectively wiped out roughly a third of the force that had originally surrounded them. Bodies were strewn all over the ground with limbs at awkward angles. There was a black dirt crater from where the stick had landed. As she kept turning in her tight circle she came face to face with Liam climbing up the cage in front of her. He didn't stop but his words reached her as he passed her face, 'Do not show them your fear. Be ready.'

Fear. She had not acknowledged the emotion coiled tight inside her gut until now. Ready. Ready for what? What were these barbarians capable of? They had come in numbers equipped with ancient technology. Even she knew it was unwise to underestimate a foe in battle. Mari continued turning until she was facing Scott's back again. She knew that she had promised Scott in Liam's hearing that she would try to escape the oncoming battle. The odds were against them in such numbers that if she tried to leave the cage she would have to fight her way through the Eighters herself.

Scott looked back over his shoulder to ensure she was in position directly over the trap door. He knew that the expression on his face was one she would not have seen from him before. Rage. Rage at the male who had taken Rachael from him. Rage at the males who were trying to take Mari from him. Cold. Hard. Rage. He watched as Mari raised her chin showing the whole world she would not part from him without a fight. He was so proud of her. She was staring death in the eyes with deadly intent. She caught his eye and her mouth curled up into a small grin. Her words from an earlier conversation ricocheted through his mind as he turned to face their enemy, 'Let them come. Together we are stronger than an entire army. We fight for what is ours.'

Mari knew that she had been wrong. They were facing something she had never seen before in her life. It was clearly obvious to her that she had intruded upon the male world. As the Eighters surrounding them hurled insults at them, jostled for position, gestured at them and mimicked indecent acts to rattle them she knew without a doubt that she would rather die before spending time in the company of one of those males. She glanced up at Liam. He stood equally as still above her on top of the cage. All three of them focused on the men closing in from all sides with deadly intent.

Without telegraphing her intentions Mari brought her blow dart pipe to her lips and rapidly began blowing darts in all directions. The Eighters climbed over the top of those who fell in front of them. When she next looked up to check on Liam Mari found that he had his crossbow trained on one male in particular. His face had hardened and his eyes were colder than the snow that had been gently falling from above.

The Eighter had Liams eyes. He was tall with faded blue tattoos on his cheeks and long matted hair tied back at the nape of his neck. He pushed forward through the ranks of similarly tattooed males to stand in front of them. 'Son.' He spoke in a deep gravelly voice. Liam did not change his stance. 'Father.' Liam acknowledged him in the same flat tone of voice. He watched as his father's gaze swept over Mari and Scott instantly dismissing them from their conversation. 'I do not see your mate with you.' His father sneered. His father had not made any changes. His vision of the future was solidifying as every second ticked by. 'You have just missed her. Christiana passed in the night. She has flown free only this morning.' He heard his own voice void of emotion as he slipped into the formal cadences of the Eight.

His father's face showed neither sorrow or grief. He did not offer platitudes to soothe his son's hidden pain. He got straight to the point as he always did, 'She was a weak mate for you. Do you have a prior claim on this traveler's woman?' Liam kept his face expressionless. He was there to observe and guide. It would seem that the fates had conspired against him to once again fight his family. He had left the Way of the Eight to avoid such a situation unfolding again.

Under her cloak Mari gripped one of her knives. The male spoke of her as if she was little more than property. 'I owe this man and woman a life debt. They are under my protection.' Liam's voice rang out strong enough for the whole mountain to hear. 'You have come to take the woman and kill her man in great numbers. I have seen that you will not win this battle. Must I be forced to remind you of what happened at Lunar Night?'

Lunar Night. Mari had not heard the term before. Maybe it was another name for one of the solstices that marked the skies throughout a season. She continued to observe the drama unfolding in front of her as another male edged through the crowd to stand beside Liam's father. The newcomer was an older more unkempt version of Liam and he bared his teeth at them in greeting. Mari could read his body language as easily as she could read a book. This newcomer wanted her for himself. His intentions were plain to all as he accused, 'The woman you are protecting is one of great treachery who must die for her crimes against the Eight. Do you not see the bodies of the men she has just killed?'

Liam sat down on top of the cage as he swung his bow to cover both his father and the new speaker. His brother was a cold bastard on his best day on his worst he was their father in training. 'Is that a challenge Owen?' He reached down through the cage and touched Mari's hood startling her. He knew she had a path to walk and it was time start guiding her way. 'I am sorry.' His words were for her ears only, 'I will explain later. Have faith in me.' He yanked her hood down revealing her pale purple hair.

The air in the clearing immediately became charged with an electricity Mari could not identify. The males moods changed immediately and she felt an overwhelming need to crawl under a rock to hide from their gaze. She felt Liam stand again the cage rocking slightly as his feet moved.   'You wish to attack a magic woman and her mate who are under my protection.' Liam paused. Mari's skin crawled at the open lust she saw on many of the faces surrounding them.

Liam knew that an open challenge was something that the Eight would respect deeply. 'Evan, what say you?' he held his fathers gaze. 'If we fight today the Eight will lose even more men. We are not afraid to slaughter them for you.' He watched the greedy look cross his father's face as he eyed Mari. He knew to outsiders she would look weak. The only intel they would have was that she used a crutch because of a hidden injury. Liam met Scott's implacable face. He had not spoken in his chosen's defense. He realized that the male was beyond talking. He was staring at his chosen who had fire in her eyes and wicked sharp knives in her hands. She would be more than a little intriguing to any male who could see her.

'Show me more of the woman before I make my decision.' Evan folded his arms. Silence descended as Scott and Liam had a non-verbal argument. Mari looked skyward in exasperation. Her voice rang out through the clearing, 'No! That is not our way. I am not contracted to you. I will not be put on display so you can decide if you want to bed me or make peace with us.' Her eyes blazed in fury. A cacophony of sound broke out around her as she stared at her hands.

They felt like something was crawling all over them just underneath her skin. She had not experienced this feeling since before her first contract. It had been something she had never expected to feel again. She wondered if just maybe she could use it to their advantage. Mari watched Liam somersault off the top of the cage and land beside Scott. She sheathed one of her knives and clenched her hand feeling the power beginning to concentrate within it as it began to build.

'You allow your woman to speak to you this way?' Evan raised his eyebrow at Scott. He knew that so far he had allowed Liam to communicate on his behalf. He smiled dangerously showing some teeth in return, 'I allow my female to speak her mind. She is right. This is not our way.' He held the males eyes unwaveringly. The situation was unravelling fast. He was aware the odds were very much not in their favor. Liam had landed somewhere to his right and had immediately moved closer to him to protect his exposed side.

They presented a united front to the male who would take his chosen from him. He had lost Rachael due to a bad trade. Mari. Mari was different. She felt almost like the missing half of his soul. She had become that and so much more. She had woven herself into the very fabric of his being. Losing her now would mean the destruction of his very existence. She had brought him back to life in ways that he had not thought possible. He was fighting for his freedom as much as hers.

While Evan, Liam and Scott had commanded all the focus in the clearing Owen had been working his way through the crowd around to the back of the cage. The purple haired woman would be his to hold. His to discipline. She would learn to keep a civil tongue in her pretty little head. She would be his to own. He was reaching for Mari's foot when he felt her bare hand on his wrist. He looked up to meet her silver eyes a split second before she sent him flying backwards into the crowd behind him.

Both Scott and Liam turned to assure themselves that she had not been taken from them in the commotion. Mari raised her hand. The energy she had building up within it had formed into a ball of purple light. With an evil grin, she tossed it casually up into the air and caught it. She kept repeating the gesture until silence filled the air. She raised an eyebrow in challenge as she turned around slowly her gaze sweeping the crowd.

Once she was satisfied that all the calls for the Eighters to keep fighting had stopped echoing around the clearing Mari spoke, 'I only used the flick of my little finger on him. Imagine what something this size could do to you all?' 'Witch.' The male closest to her hissed. Mari shook her head in reproof as she manifested a second ball of light and began to juggle them. As they flew up into the air the balls of light divided until she was working with eight balls. She tossed them faster and faster until it seemed that all the males could see were a continual stream of purple light.

Liam knew that his father was watching the scene unfolding in front of him calculating whether Mari would be worth the loss of many if not all of his males. He wished he could tell him what hung in the balance if he allowed them to walk away with her. He shook his head. It was not an option. He could not allow the destruction of the entire earth for one male's desire.

She had dug deep within herself to find the elemental energy that ran through her very veins along with her blood. None of the males had scared her. She had not flinched at the numbers she had been surrounded by. Liam knew his father would have thoughts of making her the queen amongst his people. His primary weapon he would use without discrimination against all the outsiders who constantly ran rampant through his territory.

Mari stopped juggling, allowing the energy to compress enough so that she was tossing just one ball of light again. She had no illusions that her display would avert a battle if Liam's maniac of a father wished her to be captured. She raised her chin and spoke to him directly, 'I am not delusional. I have been fighting for my freedom my entire life. I am not a possession to be owned nor was I put on this planet to be your plaything. I will not be used and you will not harm one hair on either one of my males heads.' Her challenge had been issued.

Arguing broke out all around the clearing but Mari focused on drawing massive amounts of energy to her from the nature surrounding them. Fights between the Eighters followed and she waited until the last possible moment to scream at any who cared to listen to her, 'DROP TO THE GROUND! NOW!'

Liam dragged Scott down with him as she released the energy. Silence reigned. Mari watched as those who had survived the blast struggled back to their feet. Liam leaned back against the side of the wagon. He spoke into the empty air, 'That demonstration is just the beginning of her power. No man will ever own her. You would do well to end this stupidity now.' Liam continued directing his words to his fathers ears alone, 'You will end the entire earth over one woman.'

'You have seen the end of the Eight in this fight?' Evan asked finally regaining the use of his voice. Liam nodded tightly, 'I have.' He had seen the deaths of brothers, uncles, friends and his father. He realized that most of his vision had already come to pass.

Evan grunted in response. Liam waited knowing that if Evan continued to call his men to him they would all die and there would be no one left to remember them-no one but him. He had hoped to one day mend the rift that had caused him to flee from the only home he had ever known. He knew without a doubt it would not be this day.

'It is time to return to the valley.' Evan declared in a voice that could be heard to the edges of the clearing. Liam met his father halfway and grasped him by his forearm in farewell. 'You will not return to the way?' Evan asked quietly. 'It is not yet time. I have seen the day that I will return. I will have company with me the day I ride into camp.' Liam replied. Nodding his head in understanding Evan gave the order and the Eighters melted back behind the tree line.

He turned to see Scott unlocking the cage doors. He shouted urgently, 'DO NOT TOUCH HER UNTIL SHE HAS RELEASED THE ENERGY BACK TO THE EARTH WITH HER THANKS!' Liam watched as Mari floated off the end of the wagon and then walked unaided to the nearest tree. He joined Scott at the end of the wagon to watch her press her bare hand against the bark of the tree and close her eyes. Purple wildflowers pushed up through the snow around her feet. Mari made her way back to them slowly as she continued to drain excess energy back to nature. The flowers continued pushing their way up through the snow in her wake.

Scott pulled Mari into his arms in a rough hug as she spoke, 'I don't understand. I don't have magic. What was that?' Over her head Scott looked at Liam for answers. 'It's something women born with purple hair can do. I had a feeling she has been drawing on the earth to help me heal since she first laid her hands on me.' He didn't care if what she could do was a gift or a curse. Scott cared that the female he loved was right where she belonged-in his arms. He held her close as she finally admitted, 'Tired. I feel exhausted.' Scott tipped Mari's face up so that he could examine it.

Without a word he swung her up into his arms and strode across to the wagon. He settled her back into her furs and blankets. 'Rest.' He kissed her forehead as Liam started to put the canopy back over the cage. Scott sat with her until her eyes closed. When he looked up Liam was seated on the passenger side of the front of the wagon. The horses had been returned to them waiting patiently to be harnessed back onto the wagon. Liam spoke quietly, 'They will be looking for us again at first light. The peace is never guaranteed for any longer. I know somewhere where we can hide.'

Chapter Twenty-Three - Sanctuary

My home was a small holding hidden inside an earth bank on the side of a gentle sloping hill. Unless a traveller approached from a certain angle no one ever visited. Tia and I had created the underground hide away after we had fled from the Way of the Eight with nothing but the clothes on our backs.

Once inside, I could finally breathe again. Tia had decorated the place so it was a balm to my soul every time we returned for a season. I had brought the strangers into my sanctuary. Mari had not returned to consciousness during the rest of the journey. I had watched Scott sit by her around the cave fire and knew they needed to come home with me.

She had worn herself thin trying to keep Tia alive and then during the aftermath with the Eighters. 'She's been sleeping for three nights.' Scott greeted me with fear on his face, 'What is this? Its not normal.' I took the chair on the opposite side of the bed where Scott had laid his chosen. 'Nothing about a purple haired woman is normal.' I repeated as patiently as I could. The man was exhausted. I had not been able to get him to leave her for more than a few minutes to refresh himself under a shower.

The environmental changes wrought by the ancestors had also affected the abilities of future generations of the human race. Scott squeezed Mari's hand gently. He tucked it back under the cover and then looked back up at me with a worn look on his face, 'I can't lose her. She changed me. I dont recognise myself anymore.'

'Your Mari will wake.' As if to prove me right her eyelids flickered and slowly opened to reveal her silver eyes. She looked around the room in confusion. 'Three nights?' Her voice cracked a little rusty from lack of use. I watched as she reached up for Scott's face then froze as if remembering tossing around balls of purple energy to keep us safe. She had curled her fingers back away from him. She had a slightly helpless look on her face and I realised she was afraid of harming us.

'You will not harm us.' I handed her a cup after Scott helped her to sit up in the bed. We watched silently as she sniffed the cup before swallowing a mouthful. It was Tia's personal healing blend of Echinacea and Sage tea with a generous dollop of honey. She exchanged a look with Scott before they turned to look at me again.

'Explain.' She looked as if she would wring my neck for answers to all the questions that must be circling around in her head at an alarming rate. I shifted in my seat feeling slightly uncomfortable. 'I think you tap into the earths energy for healing and for personal defence. Probably only in extreme situations.' I exchanged a long look with Scott over the top of the bed.

She had only just woken from a healing sleep. It would not be prudent to share too much information with her straight away. 'Where are we?' Her question broke the tension in the room. 'This is my Sanctuary. We are not too far from Bordertown on the other side of Eighters territory.' I took the wooden mug from her and put it down on the side table beside the bed.

I knew it was time. It was time to share with Mari the information I had fed to Scott in pieces while we had been waiting. Tia would have explained the information much better than I ever could. She had been a natural born story teller. 'I am the youngest full blooded son of Evan Hart, chief warlord of the Way of the Eight.' I took a deep breath and continued.

'Every storm season when the snow builds so high that the train refuses to pass through the mountains towards Sand City the Eight prepare to strike hard for supplies and women. My father likes to keep all of the women penned together in a holding cell until lunar night.' These were painful memories for me.

I had not been able to save any of the other women my father had had me guard. I had met Tia through the bars one evening. She had been full of such fire that her personality had caught my attention immediately. 'On lunar night all men may challenge each other for the right to own a woman of their choice.' I had watched many of these death matches over the summers of my life and I survived the one lunar night my name was entered onto the list.

'My father has been specifically looking for women with purple hair. Tia was one of the women he had brought into the camp three years ago.' I swallowed. My mouth was dry.'My father puts these women through all sorts of tests to determine the triggers, nature and extent of their affinity with earth energy. In short, they are tortured beyond all limits. The Eighters mistakenly believe that it is some kind of female magic that can be used against them in particular.'

I watched Scott take one of Mari's hands. He rubbed his thumb in a circular comforting pattern until she seemed more grounded. I had not noticed her becoming distressed feeling somewhat lost in my own past. Scott nodded for me to continue. 'Thaw season after thaw season I watched him load these broken women into the extra baggage car on the first train through the mountains after storm season. There would always be a message for the high council of Spark City. I never knew what he wrote.

One night I met Tia through the bars during one of my shifts on guard duty. The more time I had spent with her I came to believe that her spirit would be too gentle to survive the testing period. I knew that she was the one woman I would be prepared to go through lunar night for. I made a deal with my father over Tia. If I did not survive lunar night, then he could do what he wished with her. If we did survive then we would make our own way in the world until it would be time for me to return to the Eight.'

The pain of the past gripped at me once again and all I could do was warn the female in front of me, 'Most of the women captured had no awareness of their latent talents other than the training for pleasure. You're different and Evan will be hunting you until the day he dies. You had the instinct already and you knew how to use your magic without being trained.'

Mari replied quietly, 'I was trained. Elder Bryce was my tutor in many areas of my training. I could never tap into the energy stream like I did back there in the clearing. In fact, I believed that I did not have this skill and had forgotten it even existed until…' She looked down at her hands again and I knew her thoughts had turned to the many lives she had ended in those moments.

'You protected yourself and us along with you.' She could not be allowed to believe she had done anything other than use her gifts as they were intended, 'Someone put you in an extreme situation and you used it to defend yourself without thinking. You didn't monitor how much you had been using to heal us that when you gave the excess back to the earth you gave too much of your own energy along with it.'

Liam knew she needed more training. She was only just beginning to realize that her long sleep had been a result of using the energy so indiscriminately. There had been a chance that it could have cost Mari her life. He kept silent allowing her to process everything he had shared with her. 'You said that your father spent most of his days studying how this magic works. Can you tell me what I need to know so that I do not make a similar mistake in the future?' she asked her words carefully chosen.

I had discussed this possibility with Scott over the time we had kept each other company. He only wanted her to be safe every time she accessed her healing gifts when trying to help others. She had healed me way beyond physical illness. I believed that she had taken the emotional pain of Tia's passing from me and with it the edge of the sharp pain of grief as well. Every time I thought of Tia I felt only a dull ache in my chest. Pain was meant to be felt and some pain was meant to be lived.

Tia had been collecting information about the phenomenon over the past three years since they had left the eight. I knew that there was a book in which she explained the finer points of how it all worked. Hopefully it would be enough for Mari to learn the control she needed. My truth telling had not been easy and had only just covered the basic facts of a much larger story which I shared with Scott. 'We will start in the morning.' My tone left no room for discussion, 'I'm going to check the animals. Another storm is rolling in.'

I left the couple to their privacy. I needed space. Closing my eyes, I was drawn immediately to the future. I had managed to avert a huge crisis and yet the outcome still remained the same. It seemed as if my father was truly the man I knew him to be. He would make another attempt to take Mari back to the Eighters camp. He would not use force in this attempt. Sleep overtook the visions as my body succumbed to exhaustion.

The brown leather bound book was where Tia left it last time she had written in it. Her pen was still neatly capped lying beside ready for the next time she would pick it up to add more knowledge to the pages. It was very thick and Tia had almost filled three quarters of the book with tiny writing and diagrams. She had pressed herbs and other plants between the pages. Instead of drawing pictures she had labelled the plant after it had dried.

Mari would understand why some of the Eighter males had called her a witch after reading it.

She had curled up in a patch of light in the warmest place in the living area absorbing everything as soon as she received the book from me. I knew how overwhelming Tia's book could be with pages on convergences, white spirals, black spirals, the need for balance and so much more. It explained how the energy Mari was able to tap into was derived from the ley lines within the earth itself. She would have to study the book for the answers on her questions.

It was only my job to guide her to the book. The diversity of theories contained in the pages had come from many different sources. We had travelled far and wide as the need for a good mating tattooist was high. We had collected possible theories on psychic healing as well as many herbal remedies for the physical healing of a body. There were defensive techniques based on the ancient art of Tai Chi that had varied results should she attempt to learn them later. The book covered psychometry, telekinesis, apportation, empath abilities and much more.

I watched Mari put the book down before rubbing her temples. I had only marked a few sections for her to start with and they were a vague drop in the ocean compared to the vastness of the knowledge stored within those pages. I put a glass of juice and two pain tablets on the table beside her. 'She spent her entire life researching the why of her abilities. Tia was able to know things by touching people or objects. She could tell you where you had been, what you were thinking and what you were going to do next. She had knowledge but no defenses.' I spoke as I looked at the eerie landscape through the wall of glass, 'She would want you to keep her book. Maybe you can add to it and help unlock someone elses abilities in the future.'

I looked down at her. Something had been bothering me ever since the battle in the mountains.

'When you challenged my father in the mountains you said that you would not be used and your males would not be harmed. Why did you call me yours?' Scott entered the room on silent feet. He acknowledged me with a brief nod as he too waited to hear her answer.

'I don't know how to explain the feeling. I know that one day you will be part of my family. I can't explain my choice of words except to say I wanted to keep you both safe. I would rather fight with words than destroy lives around me. Especially the lives of males who had families waiting for them to come home.' Mari's face took on a faraway look that I recognized without a shadow of a doubt. She had been touched with foresight as well.

I watched as Scott helped Mari to her feet. She was gripping the handle of her crutch once again unsteady as she made her way around the room to stand in front of me. Her eyes roamed my face as if memorizing it for some day in the future. 'You are welcome at our hearth any time you are passing our way.' She spoke the words of a traditional farewell and yet the words felt as if they were meant for a loved one as they wrapped themselves around my heart.

I offered Scott my arm and he gripped it. His eyes conveyed to me that he understood that I was a wanderer by nature and one day I would wander back in their direction. The words Mari had uttered had been one of promise and Scott added, 'We'll expect to see you before next storm season.' I kept watch long after the wagon had crested the next hill unable to decipher the emotions churning deep within.

Chapter Twenty-Four - Responsibility

A feeling of unease settled over her as they left the hillside hideaway. Mari felt as if her whole world had shifted on its axis in the last few weeks. 'I'm not ready to go back yet.' She broke the silence as she started to recognize some of the landmarks around the outskirts of Bordertown. She knew that she had not come to terms with the magnitude of what she had done up in the mountains. The low grade buzzing underneath her skin had returned and she felt on edge.

'We're not.' Scott assured her as he eyed the fence that surrounded Bordertown. He had had enough long chats with Liam to know that the Eighters would stop at nothing to recover Mari and use her as a weapon. He had seen how Evan had salivated over his chosen. Keeping Mari safe had taken on a whole new meaning. Liam seemed to think the future of the whole world hinged on it.

Eighters had entered Bordertown in the past. Liam had seemed to think they would enter the town so that they could snatch her from the street. Even more unsettling was the fact that both Rebekah and his father had left them disturbing com messages warning that the Eighters had indeed come down off the mountains. The scanty details he had said that they had been spotted on the very edges of the open fields surrounding the town.

Scott was not at all sure that he wanted Mari to continue to wield her magic at her own expense. He wanted her to get it under her control before attempting to use it again. She had shown courage beyond measure when she had stood up to the Way of the Eight in the mountains. He wasnt sure that the townspeople would be as understanding of her abilities as he was. He did not want Mari facing any kind of persecution for being herself. Silhouettes of people showed along the palings of the tall fence encircling the town and Scott knew he wasnt imagining the hooting of the owls echoing around the fields.

The horses changed course without warning. Mari thought that maybe Scott was urging the horses to run faster. The wheels bumped down into an old dirt track that was partially hidden in the long grass. 'What is it?' she had to shout to be heard over the horses thundering hooves. Scott held the reins loosely and allowed the horses to slow down to a canter. The caves were less than a days travel away. 'I had a couple of com messages this morning while you were studying the book.' He spoke as he scanned the tree line. Mari turned her silver gaze on him as he added, 'The Eighters were spotted approaching Bordertown in numbers not seen in our territory for a couple of generations. '

Mari absorbed his words quickly. They were running. He had mentioned his family used caves in times of trouble. 'We were running to the caves?' She asked the question knowing he would only confirm her suspicions. The Eighters had seen what she was capable of. They wouldnt stop coming for her until they had her in their possession. Her face paled at the thought. The conditions they kept their females in that Liam had described had left her feeling appalled.

'We cant hide from them forever.' She pointed out quietly and added, 'They will keep coming for me unless we find some kind of solution. ' 'Not forever.' Scott agreed his eyes raking every inch of their surroundings. He wanted to keep Mari hidden until this latest threat to her safety disappeared.

Mari gripped Scott's arm to get his attention. 'We can t run from this. We brought them over the mountains after us.' She had an expression on her face that Scott couldn t read as she added, 'Let them come. Let them keep coming. There is clearly something wrong with a male who is willing to sacrifice his whole tribe for the right to possess one female.' Her inner strength continued to surprise him and Scott privately agreed with her.

However as much as he couldn't let her be taken from him they still couldn't let the Eighters turn Bordertown into a replica of the camp Liam had described to him. It had sounded as if Liam had grown up in the bowels of hell itself. He couldn't let the females he knew suffer and watch all the males be killed. Mari's hands had begun to glow softly. If she had noticed the change in them she was focusing on the task ahead of her.

'You had better learn how to control the energy then.' He tapped the book in her lap. If she wouldn't allow him to run, he wanted her to be prepared. Who knew what twists and turns her abilities would spiral into next if it got out of her control. Scott brought the horses to a complete stop before turning the wagon around slowly. He didn t like the fact that they needed to confront Evan and Owen Hart all over again. Mari didn t like the idea any more than Scott did. She took a deep breath and explained, 'The only plan I have is to draw the Eighters to me. To us.' It was a bad plan. Too much could go wrong. Looking ahead on the track she made out a lone figure on a horse. The shape of a crossbow strapped across his back was unmistakable. Liam. Liam had known they would need help.

He must have left his home not long after they did. Mari studied his face as they pulled up alongside his horse. He wasn't displaying any emotion. 'I thought you could use another weapon.' He looked at them and rested his hands on his knees as Mari asked quietly, 'Did you foresee the outcome as well?' She was fairly sure that she was looking at a male seer.

They were rare but Mari had read enough of Tia's book to recognize the one in front of them. Tia had had enough time to think about how the males received their abilities and all she had written was that the youngest son born to certain purple haired women had the abilities to see forward, sideways and backwards in time.

He swung down off his horse choosing not to answer the impertinent question. If she had read that far in the book, then she knew enough not to ask such a question of him. Her newly discovered abilities were enough to contend with without learning about his. Liam grasped forearms with Scott in greeting. 'Another weapon is always welcome. Will you ride with us?'

Liam shook his head. He was there to stand witness to the interaction between Mari and his father. Mari closed her eyes. She did not know how the day would end or who would be left standing at the end of the altercation. 'Must you bear witness to my actions this day?' she asked not looking at either male. Silence greeted her comment.

Scott and Liam were not made up of pretty words but of action. Scott wrapped her up in his arms and spoke directly into her ear, 'Have faith in yourself. I know you will do what is necessary and no more. I have seen what you are capable of in the face of your worst fears. This fight will be no different to any other that we have encountered.'

Liam walked up the track a few paces to give them some privacy. He knew that the heart wrenching question had been meant for him. He had asked himself that very same thing before he had saddled his horse and left his hideaway. The answer remained the same. He felt a connection to this couple that he had not felt from another living soul. It went much deeper than the fact that they had saved his life. He waited for a few more minutes then fell back to join them at the head of the wagon.

He waited until he had gained Mari's full attention. He had purposely not dressed in his fighting leathers but in his normal clothing, 'I will stand witness to your actions this day and any other.' He spoke the words he knew she needed to hear. She was a healer with a gentle heart who would always check on those in her care before using her abilities as the warrior she clearly could be. He watched her as she carefully touched the blade of one of her throwing knives coating it in the energy that was starting to build up in her hands. 'They are your family.' She spoke thoughtfully giving him time to fully consider once more what she was going to do.

'My family are the ones who have flown free already. My mate has gone to join our daughter to look over me from the heavens.' Liam reached over and squeezed her hand, 'Whatever decisions you make I will be there to stand witness.' He held her eyes willing her to understand that he would not stand in their defense. Scott cleared his throat meaningfully and Liam let go of Mari's hand stepping back to a respectful distance.

She stood hidden within the shade of the forest trees on the far edge of the field. They had travelled in silence preferring the company of their own thoughts. Mari looked at Scott and examined his features. 'No.' he answered her unasked plea before she could give voice to the words. He would not lose her to any male let alone one who would tie Mari to him only to use her power and abuse her for the rest of time. He watched her consider the full implications of what he was telling her encompassed in his one-word statement.

She closed her eyes briefly as she realized that self-sacrifice would not be a solution. Scott would fight to the death to keep her safe and ensure her freedom. There had to be another way. She hoped it would reveal itself to her. 'It's time.' Mari stepped out of the shadow of the man she had grown to care deeply for. Lowering her hood and holding her hands out from her sides she walked into open.

Liam stopped Scott from following her with a shake of his head. 'She has to do this alone.' Scott stepped around Liam with the words, 'That is not our way. If I cannot stand in front of my female protecting her then I will be at her back.' With those words he strode out of the protection of the trees and stood silently half a step behind her daring those who wished to harm his female to even try.

The Eighters appeared silently and surrounded them in a loose circle. Mari noticed they were standing at a healthy distance away from her. Each man had his finger on the trigger of a gun pointed directly at her head. She felt Scott turn so that they were back to back. His closeness gave her the confidence she needed and she felt as if she could breathe again. Any hidden doubts melted away in that instant. They stood watching and waiting silently for five more minutes before Liam's father and brother appeared at the edge of the field. They walked arrogantly through the warriors and stood before her. 'What is it that you want with me?' Not a flicker of fear passed across her features as she continued standing tall.

They paused in front of her and she raised her chin slightly refusing to show any sign of weakness. 'You killed my men.' Evan spoke with grudging respect. They both knew she had done so much more than just kill his males. 'You were foolish to attempt to harm us.' She countered in a strong voice and added, 'Correct me if I m wrong but your own chief told you to stand down and yet you keep coming for me.' It hadn t been too hard to deduce that Liam had held all the cards in their last encounter.

Tia had written down some of their personal history in the book and Mari knew that once a warlord had been shamed in a lunar night battle he was required to relinquish his position immediately. 'What do you know of the laws of the Eight?' Owen asked to cover his father's moment of shock. Mari heard the words *little girl* loud and clear within the intimidating tones of his voice.

Mari stepped into Owen s personal space and felt Scott step back keeping her vulnerable spot well covered. 'I know your laws.' She said softly allowing the power in her voice to continue building with her words, 'I know the ways of the males of the Eight and I know your secret thoughts Owen Hart.' She took another step towards him forcing him to take one back from her losing ground and respect from those who surrounded them at the same time. 'You covet me because I am the most powerful female you have seen in all your years. You want to break me to find out the limits of my abilities. You want to turn me into the perfect Eighter female. Maybe if I even please you well I can be assured of not being sold into further slavery.'

Owen took another step back from the female in front of them. He acted as if she had seen deep within his soul. Mari took note of the momentary flash of fear in his eyes. She laughed a brittle laugh then asked them in a conversational tone, 'What makes you think others haven't already tried? I survived them and I'll survive the demise of the Eight. The only decision before you right now is how fast are you going to leave before the inhabitants of Bordertown come out to fight with me?'

Gone was the woman who had hidden behind her males on the mountain only attacking with the weapons of metal before losing her self-control. In her place was the female of power that they had only caught a small glimpse of in their last battle.

As if on cue the gates in the town walls opened up and tiny figures on horses in the far distance poured out of them. 'This is far from over little purple hair.' Evan eyed the figures growing larger by the second with interest, 'Next time you come through our territory you will have the deaths of my men to answer for.' He gave his males a hand signal and the circle split into various directions to elude capture. Mari took special note of the black look Owen shot her way. It had been one full of revenge before he too disappeared into the trees not far from where Liam had stood watching in silence. Mari had shown them mercy even when all they had promised her was more retribution. Liam bowed his head. So be it. They had lived to be a continuing threat to society at large.

The inhabitants of Bordertown swept across the open countryside chasing the Eighters back to the foot of the mountains whooping and hollering. None of them stopped to speak to the couple who made their way back to him slowly. Liam could see that it had cost Mari to stand tall in front of his father and brothers. Her limp was more pronounced and she was leaning on her crutch. She looked up at him knowledge flickering within the depths of her silver eyes.

She continued to her limping walk past Liam and released all the energy she had built up inside her body back to nature. She took the weapons she had coated with the purple energy and placed them against the large tree roots at the base of the tree.

Both Scott and Liam watched fascinated as the energy coating slid off her knives and evaporated into the snow. Flowers formed a carpet around Mari where she had knelt and she struggled to rise.

Scott led Mari to the wagon and lifted her up to sit on the back. Liam too disappeared in the afternoon shadows with a wave of his hand in farewell. 'You constantly surprise and amaze me.' He said turning to her when the landscape had settled and the only noise they could hear was each other's breathing. She leaned her head on his shoulder. 'Thats a good thing right?' Mari asked softly.

'A very good thing.' He reassured her and settled in a comfortable position. He needed to reveal the rest of the information he had learnt from Liam while they had been waiting for her to regain consciousness after the fight in the mountains.

Chapter Twenty-Five - The Prophecy

 Scott watched Mari's face. She seemed so peaceful in the aftermath of her conversation with Evan and Owen Hart. It was almost as if she had finally come to a deep understanding within herself. One that finally brought a measure of peace about her abilities and inabilities. He swore under his breath at the thought of causing her more pain but she needed to hear what he had to say.

'We saw the Eighters in the city working with John Smythe for a reason.' He felt Mari lift her head off his shoulder and focus her attention on his words. Scott continued speaking, 'He's been trading them fresh females for their detailed knowledge for years. Somehow he got hold of a prophecy spoken long ago in the beginning days of the laws of Anna. The Spirit woman prophesied that a female heir born to the de Montmercy house would be the strongest fifth ever born. She would have blue hair that would manifest during very strong emotion. This female will have the means to shake the very foundations of Anna's laws.'

Scott paused allowing her to absorb the prophecy before asking, 'Do you think John thought it might have been about you?' Whether or not she was the child of this prophecy made little difference to him. She had shown him she was not afraid to be herself in all situations. Scott wrapped his arm around her as she looked at him blankly. He allowed her the space she need- ed to work through her history and the possible outcomes.

Mari started connecting the dots of her life in her head. She had been pushed off a balcony. She was sure that this had been an attempt to force her to heal herself by John who had only ever wanted to possess her for her beauty. Early on in her caging she had stopped healing the wounds on her body in defiance of his constant demands to see how far her healing talents had come. She would have welcomed her own death at the hands of that monster until the child had come along. Mari recognized that event as the turning point when she had begun to fight back in subtle ways. She met Scott's concerned face with a small smile. She was so grateful that she had kept fighting.

She kept concentrating. She was the only known female heir of the de Montmercy line. It made perfect sense to Mari that John would have thought that this elusive spirit child was her. She shuddered as she remembered Elanna boasting to her that she had had a son to each male she had to choose between. If the man was worthy enough she had given him a daughter also. Mari had always thought that the male who had helped create her had been the only one. What if she had a sister as well as brothers?

'I am not the last female in the de Montmercy line.' She stat- ed with surety, 'I am certain that there is definitely one other.' Scott had to lean closer to her to hear what she was saying. Mari sounded as if she was in shock. 'How?' he asked brush- ing one of her errant strands of hair off her face. She had a faraway look on her face as she replied, 'Sometimes the maids talked louder than they should have in Smythe Towers. I believe Elanna gave birth the day before I was summoned for. I heard stories of a perfect baby girl. No one ever knew what had hap- pened to her or if she had even existed to begin with. John and

Elanna had had a monumental fight. I thought my memories had always been gossip until now.'

'Is it possible that this other child is the one everyone is hunting for?' Scott kept his tone gentle. 'I hope so.' She answered him with a smile that faded almost immediately, 'If what we are thinking is the truth then one of my siblings is being hunted for her abilities as well.' He watched as she looked out across the open countryside at the mountains in the distance.

'Truth time.' She spoke again, 'Are you alright with all of this? I arrived in your life less than three months ago. You were forced into a contract, someone I thought was dead incited a mob situation, we had no choice other than to hide in the city only for John to confront us in front of the high council after we lodged our paperwork. On the way back from the city we have been chased over the mountains by a tribe of maniacs and been forced to fight for the right to our very existence. If that isn't enough we discover I have some kind of magic abilities and I am still being hunted so someone else can use me as a weapon or kill me and my missing siblings.'

She was worth every last terrifying moment she had put him through and so much more. He tipped her face towards him so he could impress upon her the weight of his words. 'You. Are. My. Heart.' He emphasized each word. She had woken him up when he had been nothing but dead on the inside. Scott continued speaking, 'It doesn't matter what the world throws at us as long as we face it together. You are an amazing female. We live in the territories. Life is uncertain for us at the best of times. I love that you continue to shine brightly despite what we have been going through. I love that even though you just coated the blades of your throwing knives in purple energy you chose to fight with powerful words instead.'

Mari couldn t help the incredulous look that crossed her face. He had seen the worst of her and yet he continued to love her anyway. Scott admitted, 'I'm not so fond of the constant fighting but when everyone wants my female dead, maimed or captured

I will do what it takes to keep you safe. I hope you will forgive me if I choose not to stand in front of you from now on. Your magic makes it unnecessary for me to take that position so I will guard your weak spot as you requested so long ago.'

She nodded as she swallowed the lump in her throat. Her emotion got the best of her and a tear trickled down her cheek. Scott caught it on the tip of his finger before leaning down to kiss her thoroughly. 'Never ever ask me something like that again.' He growled at her as he drew back a bit, 'We will go looking for your siblings when the seasons change.'

Over the course of the next two days they travelled the short distance back to the farm at a slower pace. They took time to get to know each other properly away from the prying eyes of other people. The afternoon they arrived back, Mari slid down from the back of the wagon and stood in one spot stretching out her tense leg muscles. The scene in front of her had the strangest inklings of de ja vu.

Mari watched the family greet one another once again and took note of the changes in the dynamics of each moment. Gone was all the tension, anger and negative feelings that had pervaded the day she had first arrived. She took a deep breath and Scott made a motioning gesture with his head inviting her to join them.

He watched with obvious pride as she walked with a slight limp towards the family unit. Scott knew that she was now a recognized part of the family as well. After hugs had been exchanged all around Susanna led them away from the main house. She wound her way past the huge sheds and almost to the end of the pretty little glade where his parents had made their first home. Nick stopped at the cottage and spoke quickly, 'We have a surprise for you.' Susanna fished an elegant old iron key out from one of her pockets and held it out to them. She said with a smile, 'We wanted you to have a space of your own.'

Mari looked at the iron key in her hands and then up at the

male she had chosen to spend her life with. Her face was filled with a faraway look remembering another time and place when she had first received a key much like the one she was now holding. Scott quickly filled his parents in on her strange new abilities so that she would be able to keep working on learning self-control. Mari punctuated his words by sending two bursts of energy up into the air which exploded like a shower of purple fireworks in the sky.

As the purple sparkles floated back down to the ground to be reunited with nature Scott smiled at his parents, 'I think that means she likes your surprise.' Nick and Susanna turned to head back across the yard when Mari stopped them with a small grin. She pointed at her crutch, 'You asked me the first time we met if this made a difference. It doesn't make any dif-ference. Not anymore. Not to me and not to the people I care about the most. It is just another accessory on the days when I need a little extra help.'

Afterword

Dear Reader,

If you would like to read more about Liam, Jo and Jo's brothers they will be getting their own books later in the series. Life is about recognizing what you can do and growing into the person you were always meant to be. The same goes for life with a disability. Having a disability does not diminish the way you live your life. It adds obstacles which you must learn to live with, work around or overcome. That being said, no matter who you are-you will face some kind of obstacle in life whether it be divorce, depression, grief of losing someone you loved deeply or job loss. We are all stronger people because of the things we go through. I encourage you to contact help if you are going through a rough patch and can't see your way out. The world would be one person darker if you are not here to share yourself with us.

M.

If you would like to learn more about me or my previous work, please visit:

http://buttakittin.wix.com/mysite

If you would like to learn more about Spinocerebellar Ataxia, please visit:

https://www.cerebralpalsy.org.au/what-is-cerebral-palsy/ types-of-cerebral-palsy/ataxic-cerebral-palsy-ataxia/

My official Facebook page is: M.J.Wright (@elanna11children11)

Excerpt - The Lost Child

'If I don't help them he said he would hurt you.' Ethan Smythe crouched down in front of the silent blond girl he had grown up calling *sister*. She looked at him her blue eyes focused completely on his own.

It brought back memories of the day that his mother had returned to their suite of rooms holding a new born baby in her arms. It had surprised him a little because she had not gotten big like all the other mothers in the house. She had removed his book from his lap and positioned his arms before lowering the baby into them.

'This is the new little sister I promised you. Her name is Charlotte Grace.' His mother looked him in the eye and spoke to him seriously like he was a grown up, 'We are going to call her Charli and you are going to protect her for the rest of her life. This is the most important job I will ever give you.'

He looked down at the tiny scrap of humanity in his arms trying to process the meanings of some of her words she used in what she was asking him to do. 'Ethan what's your most important job?' his mother asked him softly. 'Protect Charli.' He had replied dutifully.

Twelve years later and they both were still protecting Charlotte Grace from the dark machinations of Smythe Towers. His Uncle John had been keeping a watchful eye on them ever since his father had died. Every once in a while he would comment on the strangeness of her and how unusually close they were as siblings. Charlotte spoke only when it was warranted but lately they had been communicating with a yes / no blink system.

The nineteen-year-old with his dark hair and blue eyes silently begged the little blond to forgive him for what would happen next. 'You get whats happening dont you Charli?' He asked her. Two blinks followed by two more.

I understand more than you know. I dont hate you. Be careful he doesnt hurt you too.

She wished she could make him hear her words all the time. Long ago she used to be able to make him hear her voice in his head. He liked to pretend that it had been a game they played between them long ago before their father had died. Charli knew differently. He had grown up almost overnight and she had found his mind blocked, overwhelmed with worry. He had no room for her voice. No room to think about anything other than the new threats coming at them from all sides.

'Then you understand why Im smuggling you out of here to-night?' He continued softly,'They can threaten me all they want. I want you hidden somewhere safe. Pack a bag with enough clothes for a couple of days. Im taking you to Mercy House.'

Charli watched him get her soft travel bag down from the top of the closet. He would have to appear somewhere in the main house for Uncle not to get suspicious that he was dodging his lessons again. John Smythe was a shadow of the man he had once been but he had become even more vicious. Charli had heard all the gossip he had had a female once. She had been exquisite by all accounts and then they had had a falling out. Quite literally. The female had fallen over the balcony. Nothing had been right at Smythe Towers since that fateful day.

With a quick look backwards Ethan slipped silently from her room as she rose awkwardly to do his bidding. In their world, she was four years away from the age where a female's life changed forever. In their world John Smythe was the law and she herself knew he would never have her best interests at heart. She was an invisible. Mamma had taught her to be a chameleon and disappear completely into the shadows. Uncle had been looking in the shadows and he had seen her.

There was nowhere left in Smythe Towers for her to hide. As she added a few changes of clothing, her personal items and a favourite book Charli privately agreed with Ethan. Her only hope left was to escape Smythe Towers and pray Mercy House had the room for someone such as her.

My Playlist while writing

Bring Me To Life-Evanescence
Going Under-Evanescence
Wake Me Up-Evanescence
My Immortal-Evanescence
Rotten to the Core-The Descendants (Disney Movie)
Good Is the New Bad-The Descendants (Disney Movie)
Dancing With A Broken Heart-Delta Goodrem
Demons-Imagine Dragons
Radioactive-Imagine Dragons
Hello-Adele
Ghost Town-Adam Lambert
3 AM-Matchbox Twenty
I Want To Break Free-Glee cover
Life Is Worth Living-Justin Bieber
Thnks fr th mmrs -Fall Out Boy
We Are Done-The Madden Brothers
See You Again-Whiz Khalifa feat Charilie Puth
Hall of Fame-The Script
Hit the Ground-Justin Bieber
As Long As You Love Me-Justin Bieber feat Big Sean
Edge Of A Revolution-Nickelback
What Are You Waiting For-Nickelback
When We Stand Together-Nickelback
Lullaby-Nickelback
Savin' Me-Nickelback

If Today Was Your Last Day-Nickelback
How You Remind Me-Nickelback
If I Lose Myself-One Republic
Yesterday-Glee cover
Let It Be-Glee cover
Piece by Piece-Kelly Clarkson
Thousand Miles-Glee cover
A Drop In The Ocean-Ron Pope
Fire and the Flood-Vance Joy
Riptide-Vance Joy
Broken Arrows-Avicii
Purpose-Justin Bieber
Titanium-David Guetta feat Sia
Thriller/Heads Will Roll-Glee mashup
Listen To Your Heart-Glee cover
I Know Where I've Been-Glee cover
Light Up The World-Glee cover
Todays the day-P!nk
Light It Up-One Republic
Preacher-One Republic
All I Need-Within Temptation
Love Me Like You Do-Justin Bieber

My Playlist While Editing:

Yiruma
Jess and Matt
Chris Tamwoy
Tommy Emanuel
Taylor Henderson
Try Everything-Shakira
Human Nature
The Willis Clan